Bells, Bodies & Blizzards

A Willowcroft Cozy Mystery Book Four

Fran Heap

First published by Frances Heap contactable at fran@franheapwriter.com

ISBN: 978-1-923537-03-3 (ebook)

978-1-923537-04-0 (paperback)

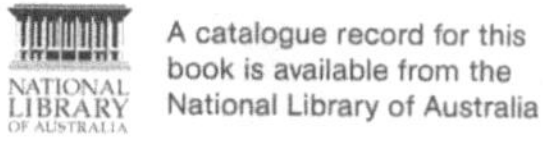

A catalogue record for this book is available from the National Library of Australia

Cover design by 100Covers.

Created with Atticus.

"Rumor runs fast; facts sometimes hitch a ride."

Mrs. Hazel Temperance

Willowcroft Map

Over the page is a map of Willowcroft.

If you would like to see this map/image in full size and color, click on the QR code or visit the webpage

https://franheapwriter.com/willowcroft-map/

If you are new to Willowcroft and need more information (or a refresher for returning readers), there is a ***Welcome to Willowcroft*** section at the end of the book.

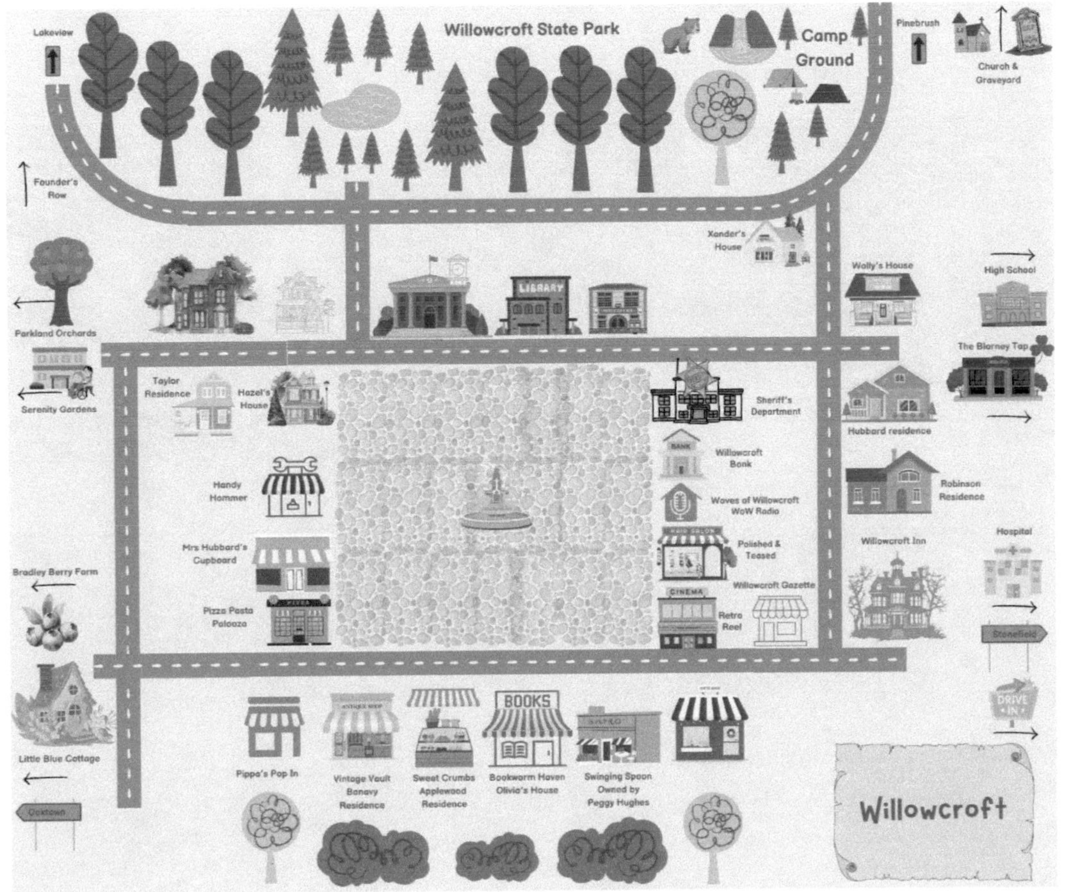
Lakeview
Willowcroft State Park
Camp Ground
Pinebrush
Church & Graveyard
Founder's Row
Xander's House
Wally's House
High School
Parkland Orchards
LIBRARY
The Blarney Tap
Taylor Residence
Hazel's House
Sheriff's Department
Hubbard residence
Serenity Gardens
Handy Hammer
BANK
Willowcroft Bank
Waves of Willowcroft WoW Radio
Robinson Residence
Mrs Hubbard's Cupboard
Polished & Teased
Willowcroft Inn
Hospital
Bradley Berry Farm
Pizza Pasta Palooza
CINEMA
Willowcroft Gazette
Retro Reel
Stonefield
Little Blue Cottage
Pippa's Pop In
Vintage Vault Banavy Residence
Sweet Crumbs Applewood Residence
BOOKS
Bookworm Haven Olivia's House
Swinging Spoon Owned by Peggy Hughes
DRIVE IN
Oaktown
Willowcroft

CHAPTER 1

Three paper cuts, two tangled ribbons, and one judgmental cat later, Tammy was ready to declare gift-wrapping an Olympic sport.

Bookworm Haven's back room buzzed with holiday preparations. Garlands draped from the beams, and tiny lights blinked their Morse code across boxes of paperbacks. A large work table dominated the space, its scarred surface crowded with everyone's projects. The room radiated enough warmth to melt any of Tammy's residual California defenses.

Olivia heaved a bulging box labeled "Christmas Titles" onto one corner. "I swear, if I find one more copy of *A Christmas Carol,* I'm starting my own ghost story."

Mrs. Temperance, affectionately known as Mrs. T, sat in her comfortable chair, knitting needles clicking in rhythm. Steam from her spiced tea curled upward with hints of orange peel and cloves.

Wally unfurled tissue paper and lifted an old bell into the light.

Lockie sprang onto a stool and batted the ribboned bell with one paw, releasing a single, clear note. Wally gave him a "paws off" look. The cat fixed him with an unblinking stare, withdrew his paw, and sat very still.

Xander entered through the back door. "All fixed, Olivia. The lock shouldn't stick anymore."

"That's fantastic. Thank you."

Tammy studied him. "When did you become a lock expert?"

"Since taking up locksport."

Wally stuck his fingers in his ears like a schoolboy. "I do not want to know."

"It's a legal hobby," Xander went on. "Think of it as a chess club for keyholes. You learn how locks work so you can improve them."

Tammy twisted a ribbon around her finger. "How did you get into that?"

"A few weeks back, my grandad had an old lockbox he'd lost the key for. He worried that smashing it open would damage the contents. I found a video online about locksport and was hooked. Within three hours, I'd ordered a practice lock and picks."

"Did you unlock the box?"

Xander bobbed his head up and down. "Inside were Dad's toy cars from when he was a kid. They're on our mantel now."

"What a great find."

"Speaking of great finds." Wally cradled a bell in both hands. "Check out mine from an estate sale in Pinebrush. Brass, 1892. The engraving is gorgeous." He angled it so the tiny snowflakes caught the light.

"What's the tradition with the bells again?" Tammy set down her ribbon scissors.

Wally's face softened. "The council commissions a unique design every year. I've crisscrossed Michigan to add to my collection."

"Traditions are the heartbeat of Willowcroft during the holidays," Mrs. T said. "And no family embodies that spirit more than the Beaumonts."

Tammy perched on the edge of her chair. "How so?"

"For at least three generations, they have provided the grand spruce for the square," Mrs. T continued. "It's a symbol of unity and continuity."

"It must be quite an honor for the family," Tammy said.

Wally placed a gentle hand on Tammy's shoulder. "There's plenty to hear about the Beaumonts. They're as much a part of this town as the cobblestones." The spark faded from his eyes. "But here's the twist. The current head of the Beaumont family, Archibald, is known as the town's biggest humbug."

Tammy's hands froze mid-wrap. "You're kidding! But the tradition—"

Wally smirked. "Continues without fail, despite Archie's notorious disdain for all things merry. Quite the paradox."

"But if he hates Christmas, why bother?"

"Some traditions outweigh feelings," Wally said as he polished his bells. "It's not always about the joy. Sometimes it's about honoring the past and maintaining connections."

Mrs. T set her knitting aside. "He wasn't always that way. In fact, no one loved Christmas more. He and his grandfather would spend hours decorating, singing, and larking around."

"What changed?"

Mrs. T sighed. "His grandfather passed away. It hit him hard, especially when Christmas came around. He just... stopped believing. Like the light had gone out of him."

Wally cleared his throat. "But still, every year, a Beaumont spruce stands tall in the square."

Olivia shifted her box aside. "He's honoring his grandfather's memory, even if he doesn't celebrate himself."

Tammy drew a slow breath. Some air would do her good. And if she didn't get her grandfather's gift in the mail today, she'd never hear the end of it.

"Speaking of the spirit of the season, I need to get this parcel on its way."

The snowshoes betrayed Tammy again.

She floundered through the fresh powder, each clumsy step throwing a puff of frost into the crisp air. The parcel, festooned with cheerful holiday stickers, wobbled in her grip. Christmas lights adorned the lampposts and storefronts, casting a magical glow as *Let It Snow! Let It Snow! Let It Snow!* drifted from hidden speakers.

Lockie surfaced from her roomy tote bag, whiskers twitching at the cold. Smart cat. He refused to set paw in this white nightmare.

"Almost there."

It had snowed on and off for weeks already, and she still wasn't used to it. LA had never prepared her for sub-zero temperatures.

Tammy absorbed the festive scene before her. The town square was transforming into a snow globe, with icicles dangling from eaves and fairy lights twinkling through a veil of gently falling flakes. The cobblestones wore a white quilt, scuffed by boot tracks as volunteers moved about.

The massive Christmas spruce stood in the corner in front of the Thanksgiving Thankfulness Tree. It was half-dressed, with ladders propped in its branches and tubs of ornaments on the stones. The fountain held the center as always, catching the pale afternoon light. Around the edges, the European-style market was still coming together, with wooden booths waiting for signs and only a handful of garlands strung. Extension cords trailed between heaters and generators. A vendor testing a mulled wine urn lifted the lid, sending spiced steam curling into the cold air.

She shouldered open the heavy door of the post office. Warmth enveloped her. Vanilla. Pine. A gust kicked back from the doorway and dusted flakes across Lockie's shoulders.

Red and green lights transformed the usually austere space into a festive wonderland. A miniature Christmas village perched atop the counter. Tiny ice skaters circled a frozen pond, and a train chugged between frosted houses.

Lockie sprang from the tote to the floor and shot past her. He shook out his fur with theatrical disgust. Tammy stumbled after him, the oversized footwear suddenly treacherous on the slick linoleum.

"Whoa there." She windmilled her arms for balance. Her package teetered. "Note to self: grace and poise are not compatible with winter gear."

Mr. Taylor's distinctive gravelly voice drifted from behind the counter, nearly drowned out by *Here Comes Santa Claus Right Down Santa Claus Lane* playing on the radio.

"Not another one. Thirty years, and they keep on coming."

Tammy's attention sharpened. Another what? Letter? What letter could cause such consternation? Fan mail for a reclusive author? Coded messages for a secret society?

Her foot slipped again. She grabbed the counter, her package sliding toward the edge.

"Everything okay there, Miss Rumbelow?" Mr. Taylor peered over his wire-rimmed glasses.

"Just peachy." She forced a smile. "Still mastering these contraptions. They're... unpredictable."

"They weren't designed for indoor use."

She wasn't staying long. Taking them off and putting them back on seemed pointless.

Lockie trilled as he jumped onto the counter. Mr. Taylor's frown softened at the sight of the cat.

"Well, hello there, little fella." He scratched Lockie behind the ears. The cat purred, momentarily distracting the postmaster from his frustration.

Tammy seized her opportunity. "So, what's this about another one?" She nodded toward a pile of letters beside him. "Anything unusual?"

Mr. Taylor hesitated, his shoulders dropping. "Nothing for you to worry about, Miss Rumbelow. An old conundrum that resurfaces every Christmas."

"Sounds intriguing."

"Don't go getting ideas for your books. This town's got enough secrets without you digging up any more."

The corners of her mouth lifted as she focused on the recurring timeline and witnesses who'd remember. Lockie blinked once, meaning he'd already filed it under leads.

"Mr. Taylor, how about we get this mailed, and you tell me about those mysterious letters?" She set the parcel on the scale and nudged it his way.

Tinsel along the window caught the afternoon light and cast festive shadows across his face as he chewed the inside of his cheek.

"I don't know, Miss Rumbelow."

She rested her forearms on the counter. "Indulge me."

He weighed the bundle and tapped at the screen. "You're persistent."

Lockie rumbled in agreement. She scooped him up and buried her face in soft fur to hide her grin. "Part of my charm."

Mr. Taylor's hands stilled above the letter in question. "These letters. They've been coming for years, always around Christmas. Always to the same non-existent person."

She hugged Lockie closer. Non-existent? Long-lost relative? Secret admirer? Something sinister?

"Thirty years, to be exact. Never figured out who's sending them or why."

Lockie hopped back to the counter, tail swishing.

Mr. Taylor tapped the letter. "Every December. Always addressed to 'Jeremiah, Willowcroft.' No street name. Just two words."

"And there's no Jeremiah in town?"

"Not one. Someone's playing an elaborate prank on the postal service."

"But why? Who would keep it up for so long?"

Mr. Taylor shrugged. Bells on his reindeer-patterned sweater tinkled softly. "That's the million-dollar question. Each year, I hope it'll be the last, but come December..." He gestured helplessly.

"Well, if there's one thing I've learned as a mystery writer, it's that all puzzles have a solution. This one might be worth solving."

She was already plotting a novel.

"Have you ever... opened one?"

He recoiled. His elbow clipped the holiday stamp display, and the little stand rocked. "Good heavens, no! That would break every policy we have, Miss Rumbelow. I could lose my job, or worse!"

Tammy winced. Lockie head-butted her chin.

"Right, of course. I didn't mean to suggest... Thirty years is a long time to wonder."

Mr. Taylor's thumb traced the counter's edge. He glanced around the festively decorated post office, checking for eavesdroppers. "Between you and me, I'd be lying if I said I wasn't curious. My wife, Margaret, is desperate to know what they say. But I'm meant to follow the rules, and I've got a pension to think about."

"It's such a fascinating mystery, though. Agatha Christie with candy canes and Christmas lights." She bit her lower lip. "So where are they?"

His shoulders slumped. "We have a sort of... unofficial Dead Letter Office here in Willowcroft. My wife's idea so we could keep the letters. She always called them little ghosts of Christmas past. She couldn't bear to send them to the Mail Recovery Center, where they'd vanish into the system. Not exactly regulation, but... Grand Rapids forgets we exist most days. We've kept this place ticking along for decades. It's me, Margaret, and our casual driver, Paul. No inspectors. Never had an audit."

"A Dead Letter Office? Here?" Dusty file cabinets and buried secrets danced in her head like sugar plum fairies.

"Don't get too excited. It's not as glamorous as it sounds." He gestured toward the back. "More like the bottom drawer of an old filing cabinet in the storage room. That back room's about as private as it gets. Only Margaret and I have access. Paul never goes past the counter."

Static crackled behind her ribs. A treasure trove of clues, right here in Willowcroft! She could already imagine Olivia's enthusiasm, Wally's skepticism, Mrs. T's sage wisdom, and Xander asking, "Why didn't they email?" when she shared this with the team.

"Mr. Taylor, would it be possible for me to see the letters?"

His eyes widened in alarm. "Oh, I don't know about that. Not exactly... protocol."

"So, no return address?"

"Just a name—'Gwendolyn.'"

"Whoever's sending them must have a reason."

He braced his elbows on the counter. "That's what the missus says. She's got all sorts of theories."

Lockie swiped at a dangling bauble, a flash of red cheer.

The Dead Letter Office tugged at Tammy. Messages marooned between send and receive. Names. Dates. Motives. The team would be in.

She adjusted her scarf, steeling herself for the winter wonderland outside, and scooped up Lockie. "Ready to brave the tundra again?"

As she maneuvered toward the exit, her snowshoes clunked. The door swung wide, letting in frigid air. "If you ever need help sorting through that filing cabinet, I'd be happy to lend a hand."

He chuckled, shaking his head. "Nice try. Those letters are staying put."

She flashed a grin over her shoulder as she departed.

"Lift, plant, glide," he called after her. "Don't faceplant in front of the whole town—again."

She snowshoed around the square, gaining confidence with each step.

"You know, Lockie, as much as I complain about these contraptions, they beat trying to navigate Willowcroft's icy roads. Remember last week when Mr. Caldwell's new truck did that graceful pirouette into Mrs. T's prized snowman?"

She smirked at the memory, her mind already plotting how to unravel the letter mystery. What if the letters were from a long-lost relative, aching to reconnect after years apart? Or maybe a cry for help, a desperate plea from someone in trouble. The more she considered it, the more curious she became.

"Let's update the others."

She paused outside Bookworm Haven, appraising the gigantic nutcracker standing sentry at the front. Its painted wooden face grinned down at her, mustachioed and regal in a glittering uniform.

"What do you think, Lockie?" He peeked from her tote. "Festive or creepy?"

Lockie's tail twitched in response.

"Yeah, the jury's still out for me too."

She pushed open the door. The scent of hot chocolate and balsam from a decorated tree by the register greeted her. Christmas music box melodies floated from somewhere in the stacks.

She wrestled with the snowshoe straps. One buckle jammed, another slipped. "Weeks in, and I still need three hands to get these off."

Lockie meowed impatiently.

"Oh sure, you've got it easy. Four-paw drive and all that."

Once free of the cumbersome footwear, Tammy stood to find the cat already darting between shelves, heading straight for the secret door at the back.

"Hey, wait up!" She hurried after him. "I know you're excited about the letters, but—"

Oops. She'd announced the mystery aloud. She glanced around nervously, but the bookstore seemed deserted.

Real smooth, Rumbelow. Tell everyone, why don't you?

As she approached the hidden entrance, cleverly disguised as a bookshelf, excitement thrilled through her. In six months, she'd gone from mystery novelist to actual amateur detective. Sometimes she still couldn't believe it.

"I guess those 'write what you know' workshops know what they are talking about. Though I doubt they had 'solve real-life puzzles in a quaint small town' in mind when they said that."

Tammy pressed against the polished shelf between the true crime and esoteric sections. It gave way with a soft click. She let out a little snicker. The childlike joy of stepping into Narnia never got old. Lockie disappeared through the gap. The door opened to reveal the cozy back room that had become the team's hidden lair. Since moving to Willowcroft, they'd already solved multiple mysteries together in this room.

Time to see what the team makes of the postal conundrum.

CHAPTER 2

"You'll never guess what Mr. Taylor told me at the post office." Tammy closed the secret door behind her.

Mrs. T's needles froze. "Oh? You have that look."

"Mr. Taylor mentioned mysterious letters arriving every Christmas for thirty years."

Olivia's head popped out of a box. "Mysterious letters? Addressed to whom?"

"That's the thing. They're all for someone named Jeremiah. No last name, no address apart from Willowcroft."

"Intriguing." Olivia shoved her unpacking aside.

"He keeps them in an unofficial 'Dead Letter Office,'" Tammy continued.

"Has he opened them?" Olivia asked. "Surely there must be clues inside."

"He says that would break the rules, but that his wife has theories."

Mrs. T set her knitting in her lap. "Thirty years? Always at Christmas?"

"Now that's dedication." Wally stroked his chin. "Sending letters year after year, never getting a response. They're holding onto a piece of the past."

"Perhaps it's become their own sort of tradition." Mrs. T picked up her needles again.

Tammy's mother ran Christmas by regulations, not traditions. Ribbons measured. Mistakes tallied. No surprise the season still knotted her stomach.

"That's a long time to keep up a one-sided correspondence," said Olivia.

Wally angled his head. "Makes me think there's more to it. What do you think, Tammy? Smell something brewing?"

Think about anything but your mother. She let her shoulders loosen. Her people surrounded her. The found family she'd built in the cozy back room of Bookworm Haven. She sat at the table, Lockie immediately claiming her lap and kneading her thighs.

Her lips parted. "I think so. Something about this does not add up."

Mrs. T's knitting needles clicked faster. "Oh, I do enjoy a good holiday puzzle! It reminds me of that time back in '82 when—"

"Hold that thought, Mrs. T," Wally interrupted gently. "Let's concentrate on the present case. What do you say, team? Shall we take this on?"

Nods circled the room. This was why she'd fallen in love with Willowcroft. The sense of community, the shared excitement over a good mystery, the way everyone came together.

"All right then. Let's solve a Yuletide riddle."

Olivia bounded toward the store. "I'll get the murder board."

Xander slouched further into his chair. "Seriously? We're in the 21st century, you know. I could whip up a digital mind map in two seconds flat."

"Oh, hush." Olivia lugged in the cork and whiteboard stand. "There's something satisfying about placing actual bits of paper on a board. It's tactile. It's real."

Tammy savored their familiar back-and-forth. This was what she'd missed in LA. People who could disagree and still care.

"I like our history of the physical collection and your digital version," she said. "Let's not change what's already proven to work."

Wally folded his arms on the table. "We need to start with Christmas '95. What was happening in Willowcroft back then?"

Mrs. T sat straighter, her candy-cane-colored shawl slipping from one shoulder. "That's prime time for the Willow Crafters, my dears!" She clapped her hands together, a mischievous grin spreading across her face. "Between us, we know every soul who was in town then."

"We haven't got much time before people scatter for their holiday plans." Olivia returned to her box of books, pulling out another worn paperback.

"I'll be heading back to Boston to celebrate with the grandkids." Wally sat taller.

Olivia sighed. "And I'll be in New York."

A sharp pang pierced Tammy's chest at the mention of family visits. She stroked Lockie's ears.

Wally drummed his fingers on the table. "We've got a looming deadline. We'd better get started."

CHAPTER 3

Olivia sprang to the murder board. "What do we know?"

She wrote "thirty years," "Jeremiah," and "Gwendolyn." The names sat there, waiting to reveal their secrets.

"There's not much to go on," Wally said.

"And there aren't any Jeremiahs in town?" Xander asked.

"Not that I can recall," said Mrs. T. "And Mr. Taylor would know if one existed."

"And no Gwendolyns either?" confirmed Tammy.

"Nope. Not in my time."

The names rolled off Olivia's tongue, somehow familiar.

She shut her eyes for a moment. She'd seen the name somewhere.

A weathered tombstone.

Her head snapped up. "The cemetery!" Lockie startled from his nap as Olivia's hand knocked against the board. "I saw a Jeremiah when researching for the Hendersons. On one of the older gravestones."

Everyone turned toward her. The same thrill she got discovering rare first editions surged through her chest. "Who's up for a field trip?"

Xander jerked back. "That's a bit... morbid."

Olivia grabbed her coat. "Don't let it rattle your bones."

The others groaned.

"This could crack the case wide open."

She pulled on her bright pink mittens.

Tammy shot her a look. "You think a gravestone's going to solve our mystery?"

"It's a lead." Olivia pushed her glasses straight. "I remember where the stone was. Roughly."

Mrs. T chortled. "My, my. I haven't seen you this fired up since you signed Xander up for the comedy show."

"Don't remind me." He shook his head. "I don't want any part in this. I'm staying put."

"Perfect." Olivia winked. "Someone needs to guard our investigation hub."

"Don't worry." Xander pulled a small padlock from his hoodie pocket and clicked it shut. "No one's getting past me."

Olivia rolled her eyes. "Please don't lock yourself *in* again."

"Once. That happened *once.*"

She turned to Tammy. "Coming?"

"You two go," Mrs. T said.

"Bundle up, ladies. Colder than a polar bear's toenails out there," Wally added.

"Jeremiah and Gwendolyn, what secrets are you hiding?" Olivia whispered.

Tammy snickered. "Talking to yourself is the first sign of madness."

"Or genius," Olivia shot back.

They yanked on their coats and stepped into the December bite. Tammy reached for her snowshoes.

"You don't need those. We could walk fifteen minutes, or drive five."

"Drive." Tammy let them fall back into the crate.

They headed out to the car. The heater thumped to life as Olivia pulled away, rolling through town and past the state park campsite.

Olivia eased to the curb beside the cemetery. She cut the engine, and they climbed out, the doors thudding in the cold. A short path led to the wrought-iron entrance, its intricate metalwork rimed with frost that glittered in the pale winter sun. She grasped the icy handle and pushed. The hinges groaned.

"Well, that's not ominous at all." Tammy's breath formed clouds in the frigid air.

"It's a cemetery. Ominous is the default setting."

They stepped inside. The gate clanged shut behind them. Headstones marched in rows ahead, a quiet record of lives gone.

"Jeremiah and Gwendolyn, here we come," she murmured.

Tammy stumbled and caught herself on Olivia's arm. "You need to stop with the self-narration. It's creeping me out."

"Sorry, occupational hazard of a bookworm. Now, let's see what this place is hiding."

"Where do we start?"

Olivia's mittened hands made the task clumsy as she fished her genealogy notebook from her coat pocket. The leather-bound book was soft with use, its pages crinkled and dotted with coffee stains.

"You treat that thing like it's the Holy Grail," Tammy huffed.

"More like the Rosetta Stone of Willowcroft's secrets." Olivia flashed a grin. "Now, let's begin our grave adventure."

Tammy groaned at the pun.

Olivia was already scanning the white landscape. "Watch for clues."

"How about a cat?" Tammy pointed ahead.

Olivia followed Tammy's outstretched finger. There, perched atop a weathered gravestone, sat Lockie.

"How in the name of Sherlock Holmes did he get here?" The words tumbled out. The feline was still at the bookstore when they left. Wasn't he? Had he slipped into the backseat without her noticing?

As they approached, the cat meowed, his tail swishing back and forth, sweeping the thin powder beneath him.

"Jeremiah Lund, 1850-1920." She brushed the engraved letters with her mittened thumb. "And Gwendolyn *Beaumont* Lund, 1855-1929."

Tammy straightened. "As in the Christmas tree Beaumonts?"

"Maybe. But look at the stone. It's old, yes, but..."

"Clean. No moss, no lichen, with a light dusting."

Olivia filled three lines of her notebook in rapid succession. "This isn't a forgotten grave. Someone's been visiting and maintaining it."

Lockie jumped down from Jeremiah's headstone to weave between their legs.

"But why?" Tammy tucked her hands into her pockets. "Why would someone care so much after a century?"

Olivia paused her writing. "That, my dear Watson, is precisely what we need to find out."

"When did you become Sherlock?"

A gust of wind whipped through the cemetery, sending snowflakes dancing around them. Olivia pulled her coat tighter.

"We should head back," Tammy suggested. "Before we turn into icicles."

Olivia took a photo of the headstone.

"It's romantic, isn't it? Two people, separated by death decades ago, but still connected through the letters."

Tammy quirked an eyebrow. "Or weird? Who writes to dead people?"

"A bit of both, perhaps. But you have to admit, it's intriguing."

A crow let out a harsh caw. Olivia flinched. Maybe it was the setting, but the prickle at her neck said someone was watching.

"Are you getting creepy vibes?" Tammy asked, her gaze darting around the cemetery.

A twig snapped. Olivia pivoted hard right. Her mittened hands clenched. "Did you hear that?" She edged closer to a weathered gravestone a few yards away.

A shadowy figure ducked behind a nearby mausoleum.

"I don't think we are alone."

"What?"

"Over there." Olivia pointed. The tip of her pink mitten vibrated. "I swear I saw someone."

They stood silent. Still. The only movement was the swaying of the trees in the wind.

"Maybe it was a trick of the light?" Tammy suggested.

"I know what I saw. We were being watched."

The heater hummed against the December chill that clung to their coats, but neither spoke. Lockie slept curled in Tammy's lap.

Olivia parked behind the store. The back door gave way under her hand without sticking. Tammy followed her into the back room.

Xander grabbed a freshly printed page from the printer. "Got the photo you sent." He slapped a magnet over it, fixing it to the whiteboard side of the murder board beside a cemetery map with the grave marked in red.

Olivia dropped into her chair. The Beaumont connection simmered, thickening with each new detail.

"We have Jeremiah Lund and Gwendolyn Beaumont Lund buried to-gether. Someone visits their grave and may have been there just now. The letters have arrived every Christmas since 1995, sixty-six years after they both died."

Wally scooted closer. "You think the letters are meant for them?"

Mrs. T folded her hands in her lap. "They've been gone so long that there isn't even anyone at Serenity Gardens care facility who would remember them. Not personally."

"Maybe it's a family tradition," Wally said. "A way of honoring ancestors."

Xander crossed his arms. "That doesn't explain the missing return addresses or all the cloak-and-dagger."

Tammy gestured toward Olivia. "We already know the Beaumonts and Archie have a complicated relationship with Christmas."

Olivia pushed herself up and paced the room. Two prongs. Attack from both sides.

"First, we dig into Lund and Beaumont history. Find anything that burned, curdled, or went off. Second, we work out who tends those graves. Whoever cleans that stone might be who the letters are meant for."

Xander swiveled his laptop. "I can check cemetery security. Pull CCTV if there is any."

His fingers flew across the keys. The frown arrived fast. "Nothing. They're old school."

He paused, then straightened. "What if I borrow some of Ranger Dad's wildlife cameras? That's Ranger Dan to you guys. I could place them discreetly. Motion-triggered. Night vision. We'd catch the grave's caretaker."

"That could work," Tammy said.

Wally planted his forearms on the table. "You ask first. He needs to know where his gear is going."

"Of course," Xander said.

Olivia tapped the whiteboard, tasting a new idea. "What if Jeremiah and Gwendolyn are code names? False identities for forbidden lovers. Using aliases would keep reputations intact in a small town."

She grabbed a sticky note and wrote, "Current Jeremiah and Gwendolyn—secret lovers?" She smoothed it onto the board.

Mrs. T stood and collected her coat. "It's time you were at home, Xander. You can talk to your father over dinner, then get some study in for your upcoming finals."

Wally pushed back from the table. "Good idea. Let's pick this up again tomorrow."

"I'll need your expertise, Mrs. T." Olivia capped the marker. "Remember everything you can about the Beaumonts, and we'll dig deep."

One by one, they filtered out, leaving Olivia alone with a murder board that offered more questions than answers.

The Beaumont estate sat on Founder's Row. Were they a founding family?

Olivia crossed to her genealogy nook beneath the stairs. Leather-bound volumes and labeled files crowded the shelves.

She cracked open the thick history of Willowcroft. The pages whispered as she turned them.

"Beaumont... Beaumont... here. Griffin Beaumont."

She flipped to 'L.' Her pulse kicked up a notch.

"Well, butter my biscuits."

The Lunds were one of Willowcroft's earliest settlers alongside the Beaumonts. Danish in origin, they arrived in the early 1800s. They built the first sawmill along the river.

A start, but the more recent connection would have to wait until tomorrow.

CHAPTER 4

Olivia stood in the doorway of her bookstore. Children pelted each other with snowballs in the square. Merriment ricocheted off the brick storefronts, their festive window displays twinkling in the morning light. She sipped her coffee and let the crisp December air sting her lungs.

"Take that, Jimmy!" a young boy shouted, lobbing a particularly large ball.

"Now that's what I call a snow-stopping performance." She snorted, unbothered that no one was around to appreciate it.

A group of boisterous teenagers barreled in, their eyes locked on the towering nutcracker stationed beside Bookworm Haven.

"Oh, biscuits." Her stomach clenched. "This can't be good."

The teens whooped and hollered, packing snowballs with lightning speed.

Splat!

Splat!

Splat!

The balls hammered the figure.

"Wait!" She waved her arms. "Not the—"

Her words drowned in a barrage of white. The snow pelted the statue from all angles, a relentless assault that sent it careening backward.

CRASH!

The nutcracker punched through the front window. Glass exploded inward, macabre wind chimes raining down on her carefully arranged holiday display.

She gaped at the hole. Groans rose from the gathered children. The teens shuffled their feet.

"Aw jeez, sorry Miss Huddlestone!" The ringleader scuffed his boot against the pavement. "Total accident!"

"Well. I guess you could say that the nutcracker 'cracked' under pressure."

Silence.

"It's all right, kids. Accidents happen. Though maybe next time, aim for something a little less breakable?"

The teens scattered. Olivia surveyed the damage. Shards everywhere, the painted soldier sprawled across her threshold, and her fifth broken window this year.

Fifth time's the charm?

Mrs. Applewood appeared with her husband from Sweet Crumbs bakery next door. He bent to lift the fallen guard and grunted. A tall man in a dark wool coat stepped from the gathering crowd and took the other shoulder. Together, the two men heaved it upright and eased it back against the wall.

"Much obliged," Mr. Applewood puffed out the words.

"Happy to help." The stranger gave Olivia a quick, polite nod, adjusted a worn messenger bag, and retreated.

Mr. Applewood patted the wooden arm. "Good as new!"

"At least something is. Thank you."

She fetched her phone. Her fingers moved on autopilot, dialing the number she'd memorized without meaning to.

"The Glazy Leeman."

Mike's easy drawl tripped her pulse. She shoved the feeling down where it belonged.

"Mike, it's Olivia. I hope you're hungry for some window-fixing déjà vu because we've got another shattered pane situation at Bookworm Haven."

"Ah, my favorite repeat customer!"

His grin came through the line. Heat crawled up her neck. She cleared her throat. "Oh please. I'm practically your VIP customer. Maybe we should discuss a loyalty program? Buy two repairs, get the third free?"

Morning light streamed through the jagged opening, refracting through the remaining shards. Crimson, sapphire, and emerald splashed across the hardwood floor.

"Would you look at that," she breathed. "My bookstore's throwing its own little disco party."

"What's that?"

"Nothing. Just admiring the unexpected show courtesy of our latest mishap. Think you can work your magic before the holiday rush hits?"

"For you, Olivia? Always. I did a bulk order in your size after the third smash. I'll be there in a jiffy."

She pocketed the phone and grabbed the cleanup kit. A "Careful: Glass" sign went in the window frame.

The largest shards went into a box.

The broom gathered smaller pieces from the shelves to the door. Dustpan, bin, repeat.

She brushed snow from the threshold and checked the clock.

She smoothed her hair.

Checked the clock again.

Boots crunched on the sidewalk.

"Starting to think you enjoy seeing me," said Mike.

"You caught me. I'm secretly a glass-smashing mastermind, hell-bent on monopolizing your time."

"I knew it!" He set his toolbox down near the broken pane. "Though, I have to say, if you wanted to spend more time with me, you could've simply asked me out for coffee."

Her stomach flipped. She busied herself with the nearest shelf. "And miss out on all this excitement? Never."

Mike shook his head, that grin still in place. "All right, you adrenaline junkie. Let's get this window fixed before you freeze to death in here."

"I'm thinking of renaming the store 'Bookworm's Demolition Haven.' Catchy, yeah?"

"A bestseller for sure." His eyes crinkled at the corners. "Though I'd hate to see what your insurance premiums would be."

He crouched beside his toolbox. Olivia lingered on his chiseled jawline, his confident hands, the flannel shirt that hugged him perfectly.

Stop it. Now is not the time to ogle the town's glazier.

She tore her attention away and rearranged a display of romance novels. The irony wasn't lost on her.

"You might want to consider upgrading your windows," Mike said. "These old frames aren't doing you any favors."

"Upgrade? To what, bulletproof?"

Mike's dimples deepened. "Not that extreme. I'm thinking tempered. If it does break, the pieces are small and stay close to the impact."

"Fascinating. Tell me more about this magical glass that won't turn my bookstore into a danger zone every time a snowball or toddler goes rogue."

His tools scratched against the windowpane, creating a soothing rhythm.

"There's also laminated safety glazing. It has a plastic interlayer that holds everything together even when shattered. No more sparkly confetti all over your bestsellers."

"Holding together even when shattered." The words tumbled out before she could stop them. "Sounds like Archie Beaumont."

Mike paused. "Come again?"

She waved her hand. "Oh, just marinating on some local gossip. You know how juicy small-town secrets can be. A perfectly simmered stew. Rich, complex, and sometimes hard to swallow."

"Only you could make drama sound appetizing." He surveyed his work. "Could you hold this for me?"

Olivia moved closer. Their fingers brushed as she reached for the level. Electricity shot through her hand, up her arm. The tool wobbled.

"Steady there."

His dimples appeared again. Her cheeks burned.

Get it together, Huddlestone. He's just being nice. It's his job.

"You okay there?"

"Y-yeah, I'm fine." She gripped the level tighter. "Just a little static shock, I guess."

Right. Because that's what makes your stomach flip.

"Static shock, huh?" Tammy's words drifted from behind her. "Is that what we're calling it these days?"

Olivia shot her friend a glare. Lockie trotted over from wherever he'd been hiding, weaving between Mike's toolbox to inspect the repair work. He let out a soft rumble of approval.

"That should do it." Mike stepped back. "You're all set. I'll order specialty glass and new frames for the next one."

Olivia busied herself with another display, desperate for something to do with her hands that didn't involve dropping things or touching Mike Leeman.

Tammy's glare bored into her back.

It was nothing. Two people doing business. Nothing more.

Mike packed up his tools. Olivia repositioned already well-positioned books.

Tammy sidled closer. "So. That was quite a moment with Mr. Handyman. Those dimples are something else, huh?"

"Tammy, please." The heat returned to Olivia's neck. "We're in the middle of solving a mystery. This is hardly the time for—"

"For what? Reminding you that you and Mike have more chemistry than a high school science lab?"

"You're incorrigible."

"And you're deflecting." Tammy bumped her shoulder. "But fine. Let's talk about those letters instead."

Mike waved goodbye, his truck rumbling to life at the curb before disappearing from the square.

Control yourself. Mystery first. Glazier's dimples later. Or never. Definitely later.

Her fingers still tingled where they'd touched his.

CHAPTER 5

"Oh, Olivia dear, I heard the crash from my place. Not again." Mrs. T inspected the shiny new glass. "Did they leave us a note?"

"Not case related. A misunderstanding between a snowball and a nut-cracker."

Disappointment flashed across Mrs. T's face before she brightened and pulled a large, worn album from her knitting bag.

"What've you got there?"

Mrs. T patted it. "A little trip down memory lane."

She blew dust off the cover. "Come, gather 'round, dears, and take a peek at the Ghost of Christmas Past."

Tammy and Olivia huddled close as the album cracked open.

Pages bloomed with townsfolk in scarves linking arms, kids mid-laugh with candy canes, and families glowing beneath towering spruces.

Olivia honed in on a shot of children dressing the very window they stood beside, all in boxy sweaters and scrunchies from the '90s.

Mrs. T's eyes misted. "Willowcroft has always been quite the festive sight at Christmas."

A recurring face jumped out from the pages. Olivia tapped a photo of a teenager with a dazzling smile. "Wait, is that...?"

"Archie Beaumont." Mrs. T's tone softened. "Hard to believe, isn't it?"

The beaming young man bore little resemblance to the reclusive, bitter man they knew today. Olivia squinted. "He looks so...different. Happy."

"He's in nearly every picture," Tammy said. "Always right in the center of things."

Mrs. T settled into her comfy chair. "Oh, that boy was the heart and soul of the holiday season."

"What happened to him to change so drastically?" The words stuck in Olivia's throat.

"Sometimes it only takes one moment to alter a person's entire world." Tammy turned another page.

Mrs. T traced the edge of a photo where Archie stood among carolers, mouth open in song. "You're not wrong there, dear. Life has a way of throwing curveballs when we least expect them."

Wally and Xander arrived, and Mrs. T showed them the album as they settled in the back room.

Olivia explained about the Lunds and Beaumonts being founding families.

Tammy sat back in her chair. "That makes sense that the two families would intermarry."

"Because there was no one else for miles." Xander's delivery fell flat.

"The Lund family must have died out. I don't recall any in my time," Mrs. T said.

Olivia tapped her pen against her notepad. "Let's hone in on the Beaumonts then. Mrs. T, what can you tell me? Any juicy tidbits that might help crack this genealogical nut?"

"Where to begin?" She adjusted her Rudolph-red shawl.

"How about we start with Archie's parents' names? I can trace his family backward to see if he's a direct line."

Mrs. T pursed her lips. "That's easy. Marion and Arlon. Such a striking couple."

Olivia scribbled across the page. "Any idea on birth years?"

"Arlon was in my year at Willowcroft High. Class of '68. So, like me, born in 1950." Mrs. T opened her knitting bag. "And Marion was a year below us."

Xander paused his typing. "You knew them personally?"

"Oh, indeed. Arlon and I shared several classes. Bit of a troublemaker, that one, always with a twinkle in his eye. And Marion, well, she turned every head in town when she arrived. Including his."

Olivia looked up. "There's a story there."

"Oh, there certainly is." Mrs. T sparkled. "But perhaps that's a tale for another time."

"So they were high-school sweethearts?" Xander asked.

"The talk of the town. Everyone knew they were meant to be together."

Lockie leaped onto the table. Papers scattered. Olivia snagged her notes before they hit the floor and nudged him aside. He yawned and sprawled across the tabletop, purring like he'd already solved the puzzle.

"These results are bonkers." Xander jabbed his keyboard. "I'm searching for the Beaumonts and getting random nonsense such as object-recognition software, Chicago art thefts, some old federal case, a red-velvet cake frosting war, and UFO sightings over Lake Michigan."

Tammy flipped through the album. "It's called personalization. Your computer thinks you're an alien art thief who's particular about frosting."

Olivia reorganized her notes. "Maybe aliens wrote the letters."

"Send me that red velvet link." Mrs. T started knitting.

Xander rolled his eyes and kept typing.

"Now, where was I?" asked Olivia. "Oh yes, Arlon being a less common name is pure gold in genealogy work. He should be easy to find."

Across the table, Xander straightened. "Speaking of gold, I think I struck it."

Olivia scooted her chair closer. "What've you got?"

Xander turned his laptop around. "A Beaumont family website tracing back to the 1800s. They've documented every sneeze and hiccup since then."

Olivia grabbed her computer, pulled up the site, and scrolled. "This is incredible. Birth records, marriages, obituaries, even newspaper clippings." She gestured wildly at the screen. "There are links to documents, photos, even personal anecdotes."

Mrs. T set her knitting aside and peered over Olivia's shoulder. "Well, don't keep us in suspense, you two."

Deep breaths. Stay calm. Olivia navigated up the family tree. "Here we go. Jeremiah and Gwendolyn Beaumont Lund."

She clicked on a section labeled Christmas Traditions. The page filled with sepia-toned portraits of generations gathered around towering spruces.

"Look at this." She pressed closer to the screen. "Photos from 1872 through the early nineties."

Tammy pointed. "That must be Gwendolyn in the first photo."

Olivia stared at the woman. "Now we have a face for the woman in that grave."

She continued scrolling through the years of Christmases past.

"Wait." Wally shifted in his seat. "Every woman is wearing the same necklace."

Olivia zoomed in. Later color photos revealed a ruby stone.

Lockie angled himself for a better view and tilted his head as though inspecting the jewelry.

"The Beaumont heirloom." Mrs. T set down her knitting.

"You know it?" Xander asked.

"Everyone did. The Beaumonts donated the tree, organized the lighting ceremony, and Marion wore the necklace to each one."

Tammy scrolled down. "The tradition goes back way before Marion."

"Yes. Arlon's mother wore it before her. It was as much a part of Christmas as the tree."

Tammy frowned. "But if Gwendolyn married a Lund, shouldn't it have stayed with the Lund side?"

Olivia traced the lineage with her fingertip. "Gwendolyn and Jeremiah had no children, so the heirloom stayed with the Beaumonts, passed down through the matriarchs. Honor, Ottilie, Frances, and finally Marion, Archie's mother."

She hunched over the laptop. "There are no photos with the necklace since 1994."

Mrs. T inhaled sharply. "It disappeared the following winter. Quite the kerfuffle. The whole town was gossiping about it."

"Wait a minute." Wally dug out the latest edition of the local newspaper. "The 'Remember When' section had a story on it."

Olivia read the headline. "'When the Beaumont Ruby Vanished.'"

Tammy looked up. "That's when the letters started arriving."

Olivia's glasses slipped down her nose. "It is... Cause, meet effect?"

"I wonder if that was the same year as the frostbite..." said Mrs. T.

Everyone turned to her.

"There was a blizzard." She spoke each word with careful weight. "My Harold, the town doctor, was called out to the Beaumont house."

Mrs. T fumbled with her shawl. "I misspoke. I'll summon the Willow Crafters and we'll sort it out properly. By the end of the meeting, I'll have a minute-by-minute account of winter '95."

Wally's chair scraped back. His tall frame unfolded in one smooth motion. "I'll have a chat with Stanton to see if I can get access to the necklace's case file and find out if the sheriff at the time is still around for any information that didn't make it into the official reports."

Lockie stretched across the table, tail flicking like a teacher handing out assignments.

"Oh, and Dad said the cameras are a no." Xander's leg bounced. "Park equipment stays with the park. They're apparently not authorized for 'ghost surveillance.'"

Olivia tucked a strand of hair behind her ear. "Probably for the best. The last thing we need is a viral video of a ghost doing its grocery shopping in the cemetery."

"I'll check into who's running the Beaumont website," said Xander.

Mrs. T packed up her knitting. "After some studying for your finals, young man."

He groaned. "You sound like my parents. Doesn't multitasking build character?"

Soft laughter rippled through the group.

"I'll go talk to Thomas at the paper," said Tammy.

Everyone dispersed, leaving Olivia alone with the murder board.

Frostbite. Blizzard. The words repeated in her head as she added a Beaumont/Lund family tree to the board, followed by the "Remember When" article and a printout of Gwendolyn wearing the ruby at Christmas 1925.

CHAPTER 6

The *Willowcroft Gazette* was Thomas Berry's paper. The fern was set dressing.

The building crouched on the southeast edge of the square behind the Retro Reel Cinema, its awning bowed under snow. Windows cluttered with old tape residue and faded past issues revealed the newsroom: two desks, one occupant, and that stubborn plant.

Tammy pushed through the door.

Thomas Berry, editor-in-chief and sole full-time reporter, sat hunched over his computer. His coffee mug qualified as a biohazard. His hair stuck up in tufts that matched the static cling of the old carpet.

He kept typing. "If you're a press release, throw yourself directly in the recycling bin."

"Not today." Tammy stopped shy of his desk. "Gotta minute?"

He peered over the monitor and waved at the plastic chair, the one with the duct-taped armrest and homemade "PRESS" sticker on the back. He jabbed a key and spun to face her.

"Miss Rumbelow. To what do I owe the pleasure?"

Tammy pulled her best neighborly energy to the surface. "Looking for a little help on the historical mystery of the Beaumont ruby necklace."

Thomas's fingers went rigid around his coffee mug.

She waited. People hated silence. They filled it, sometimes with gold.

Nothing.

"Anything you didn't mention in the article?" she prodded.

His jaw tightened. "If you're asking about the PI the family hired recently, then I know nothing about it."

Tammy kept her face blank. *If he's throwing that out in the open, he either trusts me or wants me to know he's out of reach.* Probably both.

She picked at a loose thread on the duct-tape armrest. "Have they promised you the scoop?"

Something flickered across Thomas's face. He clutched the mug against his chest.

She let the silence build.

His desk was a disaster. Old takeout containers, yellowed notes, ink-stained scraps of paper. But nothing personal. She scanned for a tell: a sudden glance at the file cabinet, a nervous shuffle. Nothing.

She stood.

"I never said we were working together," he called.

That means they are.

His chair squeaked as she reached the door. "If you bump into any, ah... federal agents nosing around, tell them I'm not their source."

He's trying to hide what he let slip.

"Noted. Thanks, Thomas. I'll buy you a new mug for Christmas."

She stepped back into the cold. The mention of a "family member hiring a PI" lodged in her brain. If that private investigator is real, the Beaumont who hired him would want to meet away from town. And maybe it's a Beaumont tending the headstone.

A meeting place that no one would question. A grave no one else ever visits.

She tightened her scarf, already picturing Lockie prowling between headstones.

Sweet Crumbs was her first stop. Pastries fresh out of the oven fogged the paper bag. Then Bookworm Haven, where Olivia, ever the enabler of questionable plans, handed over a thermos of hot apple cider and a pair of heated gloves. She'd wait as long as it took.

From here, the cemetery was a fifteen-minute walk.

Hazel Temperance licked a dab of lemon icing from her thumb.

She arranged the drizzle squares on her mother's prized English china. The delicate forget-me-not pattern always had a soothing effect on her, reminding her of afternoons with her mom as steam rose from teacups and sunlight caught the glaze.

She draped her holly green shawl over her silver hair and carried the platter into the sitting room. Her fellow Willow Crafters sat with needles clicking. Their curiosity was just as sharp.

"Those look divine." Betty's whole face transformed at the sight of the treats. "Like your mom used to make. Remember how we'd sneak extras when she wasn't looking?"

Hazel set the tray on the coffee table. "As if I could forget. We were quite the pair of teatime terrors."

She settled into her armchair with her own cup. "I've been wondering about dear Archie Beaumont. Have you noticed how he's been even more Scrooge-like than usual this year?"

Betty shook her head. "Such a shame. Christmas used to be his favorite time of year."

Beatrice's needles kept clicking. "It's been years since that awful frostbite incident. You'd think he'd have moved past it by now."

Now we're getting somewhere. "What year was that?"

"The year of that terrible blizzard," Della Mae said.

"And the same year as that business with the Beaumont necklace." Beatrice paused her knitting. "I didn't know which blow was going to break poor Marion first. And all that a few months after her father-in-law died. Archie's beloved grandfather."

"Are we sure all that happened in the same year?"

"Must have been... oh, let me think..." Marjorie said. "1995? Yes, that sounds right."

"The whole town lost power, remember?" Della Mae pulled her cardigan tighter. "It was frightening sitting in the dark listening to the howling wind."

"Why would he go out in such conditions?" Hazel framed it as innocent curiosity.

"Teenagers don't feel the cold," Beatrice said. "Until it's too late."

Betty's knitting dropped to her lap. "If you ask me, it was a secret love affair."

The room erupted. Teacups clattered against saucers.

"But he was a teenager."

Betty clutched her teacup. "Teenage love is the best... and the worst."

Marjorie sniffed. "Spare us the romantic drivel. This isn't one of your silly novels. Archie Beaumont sneaking out for a tryst? Preposterous." Her silver brows arched. "That old Scrooge could never have been a heartthrob. I'd sooner believe in flying reindeer."

"You don't believe in Rudolph?" Betty dropped her cup onto her saucer.

Hazel steered them back. "So this year would be the thirtieth anniversary of all that."

"Don't remind us how old we are," Beatrice said.

Hazel pressed on. "Where could the necklace be?"

"That was quite a to-do." Della Mae set down her needles. "Wasn't the family at the inn the main suspects?"

Betty resumed knitting. "Oh! I'd almost forgotten about them. Peculiar they were. Kept to themselves."

Marjorie's lips pursed. "They vanished in the dead of night, didn't they? No goodbye. Just... poof. If that doesn't scream guilty, I don't know what does."

"It's true." Della Mae picked up her tea. "Georgina told me she went to clean their room and found it empty. Beds not slept in, mind you. As if they'd been waiting for the right moment to flee. The whole town was convinced they'd stolen it. My Roger was certain it was them."

Marjorie sniffed. "Same for my Gerald."

"Funny thing, though," Beatrice's hands paused, "some of the market volunteers were talking this morning. They said a stranger was in yesterday asking about the necklace. Didn't give a name, kept his head down, very polite, lots of questions. Just goes to show that old stories don't stay buried."

"It tore the Beaumonts apart, you know. It was their legacy." Marjorie's needles clicked faster. "After the theft, accusations started flying. Brother against sister, cousin against cousin. Old grudges bubbled to the surface. By the time the dust settled, half the family wasn't speaking to the other half. Henry took it particularly hard."

Betty set down her knitting. "I had no idea it was that bad."

"Oh, it was worse. Poor Arlon. He took it the hardest. Blamed himself for not keeping it safe. Some say that's what led to his early passing, the stress of it all."

Hazel's chest tightened. Arlon Beaumont had been a pillar of the community, always ready with a kind word or a helping hand. His sudden death a few years later had left a hole in Willowcroft that had never quite been filled.

"Arlon Beaumont," Betty said. "Now there was a man who could make a girl's heart flutter."

"Must we rehash your schoolgirl crushes?" Marjorie scoffed.

"Oh, hush, Marjorie." Betty waved her off. "Just because you've never believed in romance doesn't mean the rest of us were so blind. Hazel kept her needles moving in a steady rhythm. "I seem to recall a certain someone making quite the fuss over Arlon at the spring dance."

"I was merely trying to keep Betty from making a fool of herself." Marjorie's cheeks flushed.

"More like keeping me away from Arlon so you could have him all to yourself," said Betty.

Some things never changed, no matter how many years passed. Hazel could still picture them as they were then. Betty, all bright enthusiasm. Marjorie, unyielding, determined to maintain order and propriety at all costs. And herself, caught somewhere in the middle, trying to keep the peace while quietly pursuing her own passions.

She ran through the timeline again. In the span of a few months, Archie's grandfather died, he nearly froze in a blizzard, and a family heirloom was stolen. That same year, undeliverable letters began to arrive. Quite a convergence of events.

Hazel lifted the teapot. "More tea?"

CHAPTER 7

The cold bit through Wally's coat as he pushed open the sheriff's office door.

Stanton glanced up from his desk. Lamby sprawled at his boots, his ears twitching at the creak of the hinges.

"Got a minute?" Wally gripped his hat.

"You showing up with that tone never bodes well."

"Nothing too dire." He stepped inside and let the door swing shut. "Just thought I'd ask before I go sneaking around and make Bev nervous."

Stanton's chair groaned as he shifted back. "Bev promised you a key."

"She did. But I figured I'd run it by you first." Wally turned the hat brim in his hands. "The *Gazette* ran a piece this week. Thirty years since the Beaumont ruby went missing. Thought I might poke around the file, see if retirement left me enough spare brain cells to turn up a Christmas miracle."

A long exhale escaped Stanton. He dragged one hand down his face. Lamby lifted his head, his tail thumping once before he settled again.

"You know Bev will hand it over the second you ask." Stanton yanked open a drawer and rifled through folders. "At least this way I can keep track of what you're digging into."

He slid a file across the desk. Beaumont, 1995—Missing Property sprawled across the tab in faded ink.

Wally picked it up. "Not in the archives?"

"Thomas from the paper needed details for that article. Haven't put it back yet."

So Bev's key wouldn't have helped anyway. Wally thumbed through brittle pages, stopping at a familiar signature. "Well, I'll be. Sheriff on the case back then was Brown. That'd be Deputy Brown's dad."

"Runs in the family, apparently."

"Guess I know who to talk to next." Wally tucked the file under his arm, dropped his hat back on his head. "Don't worry. I'll report back before I solve it and steal your thunder."

"See that you do."

Wally didn't wait for dismissal. The cold outside slapped him awake, and he crossed toward the burgeoning Christmas market. The file pressed solid against his ribs. He knew not to ask questions empty-handed. He beelined to the coffee cart, which was open ahead of the other market stalls.

Wally tested a patch of ice with one boot, then continued carefully, two steaming cups balanced in one hand and the Beaumont file secure under his other arm. Brown stood near the north entrance, arms crossed, tracking the worksite and the curious onlookers.

"Cold one for market duty." Wally extended a cup.

Brown's expression warmed. He took the coffee and inhaled the steam. His gaze dropped to the folder. "What've you got there?"

Wally sipped, letting the heat slide down his throat. "Beaumont necklace. Nineteen ninety-five. Figured you might have heard a thing or two."

Brown's eyebrows climbed. "Now there's a ghost from Christmas past. Dad never let that one go. Said it haunted him."

A brass band setting up hit a sour note. Both men winced.

Wally waited, letting the silence do its work.

"Nothing made sense." The deputy cradled the coffee between both palms. "Started with Archie. He was a teenager then. Went missing during the blizzard, the worst storm in decades. Power out, phones down, townfolk searching with flashlights in whiteout conditions. Dad said they took shifts so no one froze."

A pack of children charged past, clutching candy canes. Wally pivoted, keeping the file pressed tight against his side. "But they found him?"

"Next morning. In the cemetery." Brown's words came out harder. "No coat, half-frozen. Frostbite so bad folks thought he'd lose toes. Scared the whole town."

"Why was he out there?"

"That's the thing. He never said. Not to Dad, not to anyone." Brown blew across the surface of his coffee.

Wally's grip tightened on the folder. "Almost sounds like he saw something. Or someone."

"Exactly."

"Mrs. Temperance thinks he loved Christmas until that year," Wally said.

Brown took a long pull from his cup, steam curling past his face. "Don't know if it was the blizzard or the necklace, but Dad said it was like someone blasted a hole through the middle of him. Never got patched up. You've seen how he turned out."

"Biggest humbug in town."

"That he is."

"But I've seen photos of him from happier times."

"Good to hear, even if it was long ago."

The band stumbled into *The First Noel.* Wally sipped his coffee while a cluster of kids built the world's most lopsided snowman.

"And later that same day, Mrs. Beaumont discovered the necklace was missing?" The question dug at Wally, sharp and persistent. "Hard to believe anyone cared about jewelry when the boy was half-dead. How'd she even know it was gone?"

"Night of the Christmas Tree Lighting. Tradition."

"She wore that ruby every year." Wally kept his tone casual.

"How'd you know that?"

Careful. "The article in this week's *Gazette.*"

Brown gestured at the file. "That's why the sheriff had it handy when you asked."

"And the necklace was taken right out of the Beaumont house?"

"The estate, yes. Out on Founders Row. Town went from relief to outrage in a heartbeat. She'd only removed it from the bank's safety deposit box the day before."

"No signs of a break-in?"

"None. Folks needed someone to blame, and they weren't about to point fingers at their own. So they settled on the Winters family at the inn."

"The out-of-towners?"

"Strange as you get." Brown took another sip. "Pre-paid for a week in cash but only stayed three nights. Kept to themselves. Never ate in the dining room, bought supplies from Mrs. Hubbard's Cupboard the first day. Barely said two words. Curtains always drawn. Georgina tried to tidy their room, but they wouldn't let her in. When they finally left, the beds were made like no one had ever slept in them."

"And they left in the middle of the blizzard?"

"That's what didn't add up. No car. Worst storm in decades. Yet by morning, they were gone. Bags packed, beds cold." Brown's voice dropped low enough that Wally had to lean in. "Georgina swore she heard footsteps overhead that night, so they were still there when the storm hit. But come sunrise? Vanished."

A caroler's high note cracked, and the gathering crowd snickered.

Wally glanced at the file. "Winters wasn't their real name."

"John, Mary, Sarah. Dad checked. No records anywhere. No licenses, no certificates, no social security. They didn't exist."

"Witness protection?"

Brown's head dipped in a slow nod. "Dad considered it. Made calls, pushed hard. But no agency ever claimed them."

His gaze drifted over the festive stalls, the lanterns swinging in the breeze. "Dad used to mutter about 'missing pieces.' He kept digging long after the case went cold. Found details of a John and Mary Winters, but both had died years before. Their names were borrowed."

The choir at the fountain struck up *Frosty the Snowman*.

"What do you think happened?" Wally asked.

"Could've been thieves. Could've been folks hiding from a past that finally caught up with them. Or maybe someone here in town helped them vanish, knowing the storm would bury every trace."

Wally studied him. "Your father was a good man. If he couldn't solve it, it must've been one hell of a knot."

Brown looked sideways at him. "You think you can finish what he couldn't?"

The question hung between them. Wally inspected the growing number of stalls, the merriment, the carols, the memory of a boy nearly frozen. He lifted his coffee.

"Maybe. I like the idea of a Christmas miracle."

Wally crossed the square toward the towering tree. Ladders leaned in criss-cross formation. Teens in orange safety vests fed strings of lights up to men on the rungs. Somewhere behind the bandstand, a box of fresh ornaments clinked against itself. The air smelled of citrusy spruce, hot sugar, and a cold that bit straight through your socks.

Archie Beaumont stood a few paces back from the trunk, hands jammed deep in his coat, jaw set. He watched the crew the way a man watches a leaking roof, calculating failure points. Someone called out. "This strand's dead, Mr. Beaumont!"

He grunted and pointed them toward a coil of spares.

Wally slowed beside a crate of wreaths, the necklace file snug beneath his arm. "Howdy, Archie. She's a handsome tree this year. Full crown, good taper. Bells'll sound right nice when that wind comes up."

He glanced at the folder, then back to Wally. His mouth thinned. "We're behind schedule."

"Wouldn't dream of standing in the way." Wally touched the brim of his hat to the crew. "Still, can't help myself. Spent the morning polishing a few of my old Willowcroft bells. Can't decide which one I'm bringing to the lighting. Tradition says it should be this year's design, but I found a beauty over in Pinebrush that I'd love to try."

Archie turned back to the tree. "Tradition keeps this town from tearing itself apart." He paused. "On a good day."

Wally let a beat pass. Brass glinted on a lower branch where someone had already hung a small bell. "Heard the *Gazette* stirred the pot."

Archie's shoulders rose and fell. He pivoted, locking onto the tab on Wally's folder again like a dog sighting a rabbit. "That stupid article should never have seen print. Thomas should've had the decency to talk to the family first."

"Old stories don't stay buried in a town this size."

"I'm not interested in the necklace." His words came out sharp. "That's from the past, and I don't live there." A muscle jumped in his cheek. "I never want to see that necklace again."

Wally kept his face neutral, as if Archie had commented on the weather. *Does the necklace remind him of that Christmas with the blizzard and the first one without his grandfather? Or is there more to it?*

He shifted his grip on the file so the label wasn't shouting up at them. "Fair enough. Once a sheriff, always a sheriff. Old habits die hard when there's a case to solve."

The man's mouth flattened. "Wander them somewhere else. My mother and Uncle Henry are the ones who want the necklace back."

A ladder rattled. Someone swore as a strand of bulbs fizzled out. Archie lifted a hand and the crew quieted. He took a step closer. "You want a quote for your notes? Here it is: the Beaumonts will provide the tree, as always. The choir will sing. The lights will go on. And the rest of it, the gossip and the digging, can stay in the ground."

"Heard you used to love Christmas." Wally gestured toward the crate of ornaments, at the old brass star waiting on top. "What happened?"

Something shuttered in the man's face. For half a heartbeat, heat flashed through, the kind that doesn't warm so much as warn, and then it was gone. "You're trespassing. Not on my land. On my patience."

Wally tipped his hat. "Wouldn't want to overstay my welcome."

Archie turned away, already calling out. "Try the other outlet. And someone tape that lower plug before it shorts out." He moved along the line, coat flaring, the crew making space as if he carried weather with him.

Wally lingered by the cord reels. Boots and stroller wheels eddied past his toes. A trumpet squeaked, corrected, and slid into the melody while a child's laugh skated across the square.

Maybe it was the necklace. Maybe it was the blizzard. Maybe it was that first Christmas without the old man who'd taught him how to haul a star to the top of a tree. Or maybe it was something else, something only a boy in the cemetery on a whiteout night would know.

He tucked the folder tighter under his arm and headed toward the bookstore, the lampposts winking on one by one as dusk fell.

Chapter 8

The cold sliced through Tammy's jacket as she hunched against the wind, the iron cemetery entrance to her left. Olivia's gloves had kept her fingers from freezing around the cider cup. The extra cookie she'd pocketed, which Lockie knew nothing about, sat heavy in her coat.

The cat prowled ahead.

"Remind me why we picked the coldest place to investigate?"

Her phone vibrated. A text from Wally said he was heading to the bookstore. She was two seconds from abandoning her non-lucrative stakeout when low conversation carried from the entrance.

Tammy dropped behind a marble obelisk. Her boot hit ice, and she caught herself, but the crunch echoed across the headstones. She crouched and crab-walked sideways, fingers gripping stone for balance.

The voices sharpened, then the wind tore them apart again.

Lockie peered around the monument. Tammy lifted her head enough to see. Two men stood at the gate. Henry Beaumont, unmistakable in his patchwork coat of waxed canvas and tweed, and barrel-chested as if he'd swallowed a keg. The other was taller, with the long lines of a former basketball player, edges softened by time out of training, sharp cheekbones cutting shadows across his face. His dark wool coat cost more than most people in Willowcroft spent on winter wardrobes.

She sank lower. They weren't shouting, but something urgent crackled in the space between them. Henry's hand jabbed toward the post, then out at the street. The other man shook his head, slow and deliberate. He slipped something into his coat pocket and buried both hands deep, feet planted wide. Not local. Not here for holiday cheer.

Tammy strained to hear past the wind. Fragments reached her. "She." "Long." "Short." "Following." "More." The rest vanished.

A crow burst from a nearby tree. Both men looked up, then in her direction.

Tammy flattened against the monument.

Henry's words rumbled between the graves. "Find."

She risked another look. The stranger turned and cut toward the street, Henry a step behind. They passed through the gate. She waited, muscles buzzing, breath shallow as she counted. Thirty. Forty. Sixty.

She pushed herself up, working the pins and needles from her legs. Lockie watched her with a look that suggested he would have handled espionage with far more finesse.

She made it two steps when movement flickered at the edge of her vision. She snapped back against the monument. Another figure emerged from the shadows inside the fence, shorter and rougher, a stovepipe beanie pulled low over his face. He skulked along the perimeter, hanging back ten yards from where the first two had stood. The moment the sharp-check-boned stranger slipped into the street, this one followed at a distance, hands jammed in his jacket, face half-buried in a scarf. He didn't even glance at Henry.

Had he been there the whole time? Was he interested in the new guy, or Henry? Or her?

Lockie's tail whipped against her shin. He tracked the third man with hunter's eyes, then looked up at her.

"Of course we're following him."

Lockie trotted forward, and Tammy fell in behind. They kept their distance, close enough to track him but far enough to stay hidden. The cold drove through her gloves. The sun crawled lower. The figure drifted to a battered red Toyota parked on the side road.

Tammy stopped. The car door slammed, and the engine turned over, exhaust billowing white. He pulled away. No glance back. If she'd blinked, she might've dismissed the whole thing as desperate entertainment on a freezing afternoon.

Except tension had radiated off Henry and the tall stranger in palpable waves, and the second man materialized out of nowhere, but ghosts don't drive.

She shivered. Had that been Henry Beaumont meeting his hired private investigator, as Thomas suggested?

CHAPTER 9

Early evening settled over Bookworm Haven. The store sat quiet. In the back room, the team gathered around the murder board while Lockie dozed on the table beside the last of Mrs. T's drizzle squares.

Tammy set her notebook down, the paper edges still curled from the cold. "Everything goes back to winter '95."

Wally tapped the Beaumont file. "The frostbite, the blizzard, the missing necklace. The Winters family vanishing and the letters. All the same storm."

Mrs. T adjusted her shawl. "And the same heartbreak. Poor Arlon's death not long after, Marion never recovering... the Beaumonts lost more than jewelry."

Xander lifted his gaze from his laptop. "The cemetery records didn't help. The Lund plot's legit, but there's no record of upkeep or recent visitors. Dead end. Literally."

"Figures." Wally crossed his arms. "Even the dead have secrets in this town."

Xander leaned back. "I discovered Archie runs the Beaumont website, though."

Mrs. T reached for her cup. "That doesn't surprise me. History was his favorite subject in school. He was one of my most enthusiastic students."

Olivia sat up straighter. "You taught him?"

"I taught a lot of people in town before I retired. He could recite the town's founding dates better than I could. Always wanted to link everything back to where it began."

Olivia tilted her head. "That explains his obsession with the past. He grumbles about tradition but can't let go of it."

"Exactly," Wally said. "He preserves history one eye roll at a time."

Tammy flipped her notebook open again. "Which makes it even stranger that Henry's the one hiring private investigators while Archie insists he wants nothing to do with the necklace."

Olivia studied the papers pinned across the board. "Maybe he's protecting the past, and Henry's trying to rewrite it."

"Either way, the truth's been sealed tighter than one of those Christmas envelopes," said Mrs. T.

Tammy's pen stilled. "We have to read the letters."

"But how do we get our hands on them?" Olivia asked. "Mr. Taylor's not likely to hand them over, even to a charming Mrs. T."

Xander sported a mischievous grin. "We'll have to get creative."

Lockie stretched out before resettling into a loaf. Tammy scratched behind his ears. "What do you think, furball? Are we on the right track?"

The cat meowed confidently, as if to say, "Of course we are, human. Now, where are my treats?"

Olivia bounced on her toes. "What if we create a distraction? I could 'accidentally' knock over the Christmas village display while Tammy sneaks a peek."

"No good," said Tammy. "The file cabinets are in the back room."

Olivia's spark dimmed. "Right. That won't buy us enough time."

Mrs. T laced her fingers around her teacup. "The post office closes at six. After that, it sits quiet."

Wally folded his arms. "Quiet doesn't mean open season. Those letters aren't ours to touch." His tone carried the weight of someone who'd spent a lifetime upholding rules.

Tammy met his gaze. "We're not taking anything. We read them and put them back where we found them."

Xander looked up from his laptop. "We don't have to read them there. I can scan two or three in under a minute. The contents go straight back into the envelopes. No one walks away with anything."

Wally's frown deepened. "And how do you plan to get into a locked cabinet?"

"I can use my locksport skills," said Xander.

"I knew that hobby of yours was going to get me in trouble," grumbled Wally.

"We still have to get inside the building," Tammy said.

"Nothing in Willowcroft is Fort Knox." Mrs. T set her cup down. "I'm sure there's a way in. Though the letters themselves will be sealed."

Olivia frowned. "We can't force them."

"Mr. Taylor will know if they've been tampered with." Tammy traced circles in Lockie's fur.

Olivia's face lit up. "We could steam them open! Like in the movies!"

Tammy pictured herself hunched over a kettle like a cartoon spy.

"Movies are not instruction manuals," Wally grumbled.

"But moisture loosens adhesives," Tammy said. "If we're careful, we could reseal them cleanly."

A prickle of guilt flickered through her chest. Breaking into a post office wasn't exactly on her bucket list. *But I'm sure it will be for the greater good.*

Mrs. T cleared her throat. "Then we're going in after hours," she said matter-of-factly.

Wally's jaw dropped. "Mrs. T! I never would have expected—"

"Oh, hush." Mrs. T waved a hand. "Mr. Taylor lives next door to me. He has a pipe on the back porch every evening. I could keep watch and let you know if you need to skedaddle."

Olivia clapped her hands. "Mrs. T, you beautiful criminal mastermind! A covert operation."

"We can use walkie-talkies to stay in touch," Tammy suggested.

"There's a kettle in the back room," Olivia said. "I've heard it boiling and clicking off when I've been in the post office. Steam—check." She jumped up and put her own kettle on. "I can start practicing now."

Xander recapped: "Mrs. T on lookout, Wally scouting outside, I'll handle the locks, Tammy and Olivia in charge of opening, I'll scan them. Everything goes back exactly as we found it."

Lockie huffed loudly, as if offended at being left out. Tammy scratched under his chin. "And Lockie can be our furry getaway driver, right, boy?"

He purred and kneaded her leg.

Their faces glowed under Olivia's Christmas lights. "Are we actually doing this?" Tammy asked.

Mrs. T patted her hand. "Sometimes, dear, the maddest plans work best. We're not stealing. We're simply borrowing information for the good of the town."

"It's settled," Olivia said. "We'll work out the details tomorrow."

Wally exhaled through his nose. "Figures. I spent half my life chasing this sort of thing." He paused. "But I understand how red tape can strangle a good lead. I'll keep watch, but if anyone asks, I'll say I told you not to."

By morning, the boldness of their plan had given way to logistics and caffeine in the back room.

Olivia had volunteered her stubborn, dented, and long-missing-its-key filing cabinet to be Xander's willing victim.

"First rule of practice," he said, producing a tidy case of lockpicks, "create the challenge."

He selected a small tension wrench and a short hook pick, set the wrench in the keyway, and eased pressure until the plug shifted a hair. A soft click. He let go. The handle wouldn't budge. "There. Now it's locked."

Olivia folded her arms. "You'd better be able to undo that, or my entire client list is trapped in there forever. If you break it, you're shelving books by color for a month."

Attempt one: a faint scrape. Attempt two: a breath held too long and a muttered, "Too much pressure."

On the third, the pins set in quick succession. The cabinet gave a satisfying click.

Olivia tugged the handle. It slid smoothly. "Impressive. Again."

He re-tensioned, rotated the plug to relock, tested the handle, then opened it once more.

By lunch, he could lock, reopen, and relock in under thirty seconds. "No scratches, no evidence, no problem."

Wally, watching from a stool with his coffee, muttered, "If I'd had you on my squad, I'd have needed fewer warrants."

Meanwhile, Olivia's steam experiment filled the store with a soft hiss and the floral scent of Earl Grey. The kettle proved splattery, leaving one envelope warped like wilted lettuce. She blotted droplets from the counter. "We need finesse, not rainfall."

Mrs. T's phone chimed, and she peered at the screen. "Back in a tick."

Ten minutes later, she bustled in brandishing a compact travel steam iron. "Borrowed from Marjorie. Gentle, steady, and quiet. Also, she says the post office's back room window is *never* shut. Isn't that interesting?"

She spread a folded tea towel on the table and plugged in the iron. It needed a minute to reach temperature. A thin whisper of vapor curled from its tip. "Mind your fingers."

Olivia snapped on a pair of washing-up gloves, gripped an old junk-mail envelope with kitchen tongs, and held it to the steam. The flap loosened. "Wow. It relaxes like pastry dough."

Tammy had turned her corner into a tiny lab bench. She'd raided Mrs. Hubbard's Cupboard's stationery section and returned with a paper bag of possibilities: a purple glue stick that promised to dry clear, a plain archival glue stick, a tiny bottle of craft glue, double-sided tape, and a ruler.

Test one: the purple stick sealed well but left a faint sheen. Tammy tilted it to the light. "Too shiny."

Test two: the craft glue puckered the paper. "Nope."

Double-sided tape looked perfect at first, then refused to sit neatly in the corners. "Fussy."

The archival glue stick went on thin and matte. Tammy smoothed the flap with the ruler, counted a slow five, then checked the edge with her fingertip. "That's the one."

By late afternoon, the table gleamed with neat rows of practice envelopes. Xander's locks clicked and relocked with crisp precision. Olivia's steam iron puffed a rhythmic sigh, and Mrs. T hummed *The Twelve Days of Christmas.*

Wally drained the last of his coffee. "You've officially terrified me."

Tammy smiled. "Then we're ready."

CHAPTER 10

The porch chair creaked beneath Hazel as she positioned herself for maximum surveillance. Mr. Taylor's house sat in full view, along with Willowcroft's square. She arranged her needles and festive red wool, her hand brushing the walkie-talkie tucked inside her knitting bag.

Snow blanketed the town in pristine white, with icicles dangling from eaves like crystalline ornaments.

A stitch slipped free. "Oh fudgsicle. Collect yourself, Hazel."

Across the fence, smoke curled from Mr. Taylor's porch. Right on schedule.

Hazel counted to sixty, her needles clicking. *A few more puffs so he's nice and cozy.*

He drew long on his pipe. She set aside her knitting and stood. Her silver bell shawl settled around her shoulders as she crossed to the fence.

"Evening, Mr. Taylor!" Cheer saturated every word.

His pipe stopped midair. "Ah, Mrs. Temperance. How are you?"

"Just dandy, though I've been fretting about the Christmas market layout. Thought you might have some insight, given your sharp sense of detail."

He straightened. "Is that so? Well, I'd be happy to offer my thoughts. Back in '87, we had a conundrum with the carolers..."

He launched into his tale. Hazel interjected at intervals, her gaze sliding toward her porch. The walkie-talkie remained silent—a good sign. *I hope the others are making good use of this distraction. But, Lord help us if we get caught.*

"Fascinating. And how did you resolve that issue with the hot chocolate stand?"

Mr. Taylor puffed with pride, relishing the opportunity to share his expertise. *If all goes according to plan, they'll have ample time to execute their mission.*

Night pooled over the post office's brick facade as Wally led them into the narrow alley alongside. Years in law enforcement kept his tread from marking the fresh snow. He raised his hand. They froze as a security light flickered to life.

Lockie's ears twitched, alert.

"Now," Wally mouthed the word.

They darted forward, their boots muffled by powder. Lockie slunk ahead, his black-and-white fur blending with shadows as they pressed against the cold brick.

"There." Wally pointed. "Second window from the left, as Marjorie said. Good old small-town complacency."

A dry click came from Xander's throat. "So sneaking in is a go?"

Wally fixed him with a stern look. "We're bending rules here. Last chance to back out."

Tammy took them in, one by one. Olivia gave a steady nod while patting the travel iron in her coat pocket. Xander swallowed and tightened his grip on the flashlight. Wally waited.

"We've come this far." Tammy set her jaw. "Time to find out who's sending those letters."

Olivia bounced on her toes, cheeks flushed. "This is like 'Mission: Impossible'! Except without the gadgets. And explosions. And—"

"We get it, Liv." Xander rolled his eyes, but Tammy caught his hidden smile.

"Nothing leaves the building," Wally said. "Xander, you're up."

As Xander approached the window, Lockie tensed, ears pricked.

"What is it, boy?" Tammy's pulse spiked.

The cat relaxed, padding over to rub against her leg.

"False alarm." Olivia's breath misted in the cold air.

Wally gestured forward. "Quick and quiet."

Were they really having an after-hours peek at the mystery mail?

Lockie regarded Tammy. "Ready, partner?"

The cat blinked slowly as if to say, "Born ready."

Xander's lanky frame unfolded as he approached the window. He hoisted himself up, his foot catching the edge. His body lurched sideways.

"Easy does it," Wally whispered.

Xander lifted again, his toe skidding on the brick. A muted thump followed, then a clatter.

"Graceful as a gazelle," Olivia said.

Tammy counted heartbeats. No alarm. Only an owl calling once, distant.

"Xander?" she called quietly.

"I'm okay! Just.... redecorating."

Olivia stifled a giggle. "Some cat burglar."

"Hey, you do better!"

"You're up next, ladies." Wally gestured. "Who's first?"

Olivia stepped forward, adjusting her glasses. "Me."

Xander's hands appeared at the window. "I'll pull you up."

Olivia grasped his hands, feet scrabbling against the wall. Halfway through, she jerked to a stop.

"I'm stuck!" Olivia stage-whispered, her legs kicking comically. Her face flushed. "Oh, for heaven's sake. I feel like Santa halfway up the chimney."

The mental image was too much. Tammy clapped a hand over her mouth, shoulders shaking with suppressed laughter.

"It's your coat," Xander grunted. "Caught on something."

With a final wiggle, Olivia popped free, tumbling inside with a muffled "oof."

"Could you be any louder?" Xander helped her up.

"Is that a challenge?"

Wally sighed. "Focus. We're not exactly being inconspicuous."

Tammy approached the window. *This is actually criminal. But it's all for the good of the town. For the people involved with the letters. Right?*

"Come on," Xander urged her forward.

Here goes nothing. Tammy gripped the windowsill and climbed.

Her feet hit the floor with a thud as Xander and Olivia helped her through. The post office took on an eerie quality in the darkness.

Olivia plugged in the travel iron. "Steam coming up."

Xander knelt, lockpicking kit in hand. "I'm going for the cabinet."

His face was relaxed as he repeated his well-practiced steps.

"You know," Olivia whispered, "this reminds me of that scene in—"

"Not now." Tammy's nerves frayed. She turned to Xander. "How's it going?"

Xander held up a hand for silence. Within seconds, a satisfying click signaled disengagement. He opened the bottom drawer.

The letters were in reach.

A faint clatter broke the stillness. Metal clanged. Tammy's muscles stiffened.

Footsteps followed, slow crunches in the snow outside.

Light swelled across the frosted window, a pale smear that brightened and shifted as the beam drew closer.

Air locked in Tammy's throat. "Someone's out there."

Not now. Not when we're so close.

She grabbed Olivia's arm and yanked her down.

Olivia fell beside her.

Xander's hand stopped mid-reach, fingers hovering.

The light gathered on the glass, thinned, then pooled again as whoever held it moved. Breath fog bloomed on the pane.

"Xander," Tammy hissed, "hide!"

He dropped behind the desk.

The beam lingered, then drifted away. Tammy counted seconds. One. Two. Three. *Don't come back. Don't look at the window.*

A man's voice carried through the cold, irritated and low. "Blasted raccoons again."

"Deputy Brown," Olivia mouthed.

Of course. The sheriff's department sat across the street. Stupid. Obvious. The kind of detail that gets you caught.

Another clatter. The light swung farther off. A bin lid banged shut. Footsteps receded.

Silence settled. Tammy's lungs burned.

"Too close," Olivia said. "We need to move fast."

Tammy agreed. Her ears strained toward the window, waiting for the crunch of boots. "What about Wally?"

"Doesn't sound like he was seen," said Xander.

The steam iron flashed green. The rolling boil of a kettle could have given them away.

"Steam's ready." Olivia snatched a letter.

She held each envelope to the steam until it relaxed. Tammy slid the pages free for Xander to scan, then tucked them back, ran a thin line of glue along the gum, smoothed the flap with a ruler's edge, counted a slow five, and returned each to the drawer. Vapor drifted in the lamplight.

"Shall we give ourselves code names?" Olivia asked.

Tammy managed a strained smirk. "I'll stick with Tammy. But if you want to be 'The Steam Queen,' be my guest."

Olivia's soft giggle broke the tension. "Just 'Steam Queen.'"

Trust Olivia to find levity in their after-hours visit.

Their walkie-talkie crackled. Tammy fumbled the envelope. Beside her, Olivia yelped, clamping a hand over her mouth.

"Knitting pattern... looks complicated," Mrs. T transmitted through static. "Might need to... untangle some yarn soon."

Tammy decoded the message. Mr. Taylor was wrapping up his conversation, their window closing rapidly.

The speaker crackled again. "Oh my, is that the time? I should be going inside. Did you say you were heading back to the post office? I'm sure whatever it is can wait till tomorrow."

Was Mr. Taylor on his way?

A whisper followed. "Red alert! Get out now!"

Ice flooded Tammy's veins.

"Go, go, go!" She moved toward the window.

"There are a couple left." Olivia's hands still worked the steam.

Xander hastily returned the envelopes to the filing cabinet.

His phone buzzed, the screen illuminating his pale face. "Wally says there's a pedestrian entering the far end of the square."

Tammy's breath caught. "Move."

Olivia's hand jerked. A letter fluttered to the floor.

Tammy grabbed it and shoved the envelope into the drawer.

"All the letters are back in place." She darted to the window.

Xander's tools worked the lock. A distinct click indicated reengagement.

"We need to go," Tammy said.

Olivia hesitated by the window. "Wait, we can't leave evidence!"

"Are you kidding me?" Tammy stared at her. "We don't have time to—"

"We've been quite naughty." Olivia attacked the surrounding surfaces, bumping the kettle in her haste. "WIPE!"

Tammy groaned but grabbed a cloth, furiously erasing their presence. "This is insane. I write about this stuff; I don't do it!"

Xander let out a nervous squeak. "Living the dream, right?"

"Nightmare's more like it."

A whistle came from outside. Olivia's shoulders relaxed. "That's Wally's all-clear."

They scrambled for the window. Tammy went first, tumbling out less than gracefully. Her puffy coat cushioned her landing.

"You okay?" Xander peered down.

Tammy brushed herself off. "Just my pride."

As Olivia and Xander made their way out, adrenaline kept Tammy's muscles tight. *Any second now, Mr. Taylor will march out from the shadows and call the sheriff.*

All three huddled in the alley.

"We did it," Olivia whispered.

Xander held up a thumb drive. "That was kind of awesome."

Tammy shook her head but couldn't suppress her smile. "You two are terrible influences. Now let's get out of here before—"

A door creaked. They ran.

Wally waved them down behind a shrub bowed under white. Lockie appeared at Tammy's ankle.

"Split up," Wally said. "Everyone go home. Rendezvous at the bookstore tomorrow. Act casual."

CHAPTER 11

"Here goes nothing." Olivia's hand trembled as she picked up the first letter printout.

The team gathered at the table as Xander added each freshly printed page from his laptop to the growing pile of copied letters.

"This is dated 2002!" The sheet rustled in Olivia's grip.

"That's before I was born." Xander passed another.

"Thanks for that reminder of your tender age," said Mrs. T.

"We're hacking into someone's emotional database." Xander fetched another page.

"We need to approach this methodically. Oldest to most recent." Wally positioned himself at the edge of the table.

Xander had scanned both envelopes and contents, giving them access to postmarks. Each envelope bore only "Gwendolyn" where a return address should sit. The printer hummed as Tammy distributed peppermint mochas from Sweet Crumbs.

This is what I live for. Olivia surveyed the room. *Friends gathered in my back room, a murder board at the ready, and a mystery to unravel. And with Christmas approaching, what better gift than a puzzle to solve?*

Xander hunched over his laptop. "Who writes thirty letters without getting a response?"

"A persistent someone." Tammy reached down to scratch behind Lockie's ears as the cat wound between her ankles. "Or someone with a secret."

Olivia bounced on her toes. "What if it's star-crossed lovers separated by cruel fate, only able to communicate through mysterious Christmas letters?"

Xander scoffed. "You've been reading too many romance novels."

"We may need to think outside the box on this one." Wally crossed his arms.

"Done." Xander handed over the last printout from the scanned post office letters.

Olivia shuffled it into the correct chronological order. "Sorted, minus the two letters we didn't get to." She looked at the top page. "You were right, Wally. The first arrived in 1995. It has an Oregon postmark."

"Read it," Tammy urged.

Olivia cleared her throat. *"Dear Jeremiah,*

The evergreen forests here stretch endlessly toward gray skies, their branches heavy with snow that reminds me of our evenings together. Each morning, I walk among these towering trees, and my mind drifts back to our cemetery, to the stories you shared, to the way your eyes danced when you spoke of Willowcroft's history. The cold here bites differently than Michigan's frost, but it still carries whispers of those precious moments we shared.

I often find myself touching what you entrusted to me, not for what it is, but for what it carries of you. I wonder if you can ever forgive my abrupt departure. Please know that every step away from you that night tore at my soul. Some choices in life come without warning, leaving us powerless against their tide. But my feelings, Jeremiah, were as real as the stone markers that witnessed our time together.

When snow falls here in the Pacific Northwest, I close my eyes and pretend I'm back there with you, listening to ghost stories and sharing secrets beneath winter stars.

Forever yours,

Gwendolyn."

"Definitely a love story." Mrs. T took a slow sip from her cup.

Olivia picked up the next printed scan. "From Arizona in 1996." She gestured toward her genealogy nook. "There's a map in the third drawer. We can plot Gwendolyn's movements."

Wally retrieved it and flipped the murder board, pinning the map across its surface.

"Here you go." Mrs. T donated a red ball of yarn.

Tammy went to add a pin. "Do we start in Willowcroft?"

"Yes." Wally pressed a pin into the board. "Willowcroft to Oregon to Arizona."

Olivia began reading again. "Dearest Jeremiah,

Christmas feels foreign in this desert landscape, where cacti stand against a burning sky. No frost patterns trace windows here, no snowflakes dance in the winter air, and sometimes this absence makes my heart ache with memories of our time together. I find myself walking through small graveyards at sunset, touching sun-warmed stones and remembering how you brought each inscription to life with your stories.

The stars here pierce the dark with startling clarity, and in these quiet moments, I imagine they're the same ones that watched over our meetings. The memento you left in my care remains safe. I treat it as something sacred, not mine to claim, only to guard. It's treasured and protected, though not nearly as precious as the memories I carry. Each time I hold it, I'm transported back to those winter evenings when possibility hung in the air like crystal frost.

Sometimes I dream of explaining everything, of sharing the whole truth of why I had to leave so suddenly. But dreams are like the morning mist—they fade with daylight, leaving only longing in their wake.

Missing you with every breath,

Gwendolyn."

"She's obsessed with cemeteries," said Xander.

"Keep reading, dear." Mrs. T gestured toward the stack.

Olivia set down the Arizona letter and picked up the next one. "In 1997 they are in Maine."

Tammy stuck a pin in Maine and stretched the yarn from Arizona.

"My Jeremiah,

Two years have passed since that magical December, yet time hasn't dulled the sharp edges of my regret. The harbor's lighthouse beam sweeps across the rocky coast each night, steady and sure, like the way you guided me through Willowcroft's history. I've found a small cemetery near the shore, where salt air weathers the stones more quickly than Michigan frost ever could. I sit there sometimes, listening to waves instead of your voice, and my heart aches for the stories left untold.

The winter winds here carry the same bite as those that swirled around us during our twilight meetings. I keep our lifeline close, a constant reminder of what waits to be made right. Of promises made and dreams unrealized. If only you knew how many times I've started to write, to explain, to pour out every reason and regret. But some secrets aren't ours to share, no matter how heavily they weigh on our hearts.

Do you still visit our special place? Do you share its stories with others, or have you locked those memories away as punishment for my disappearance? Know that every Christmas, when the snow falls thick and silent, I remember the warmth of your smile against December's chill.

Always thinking of you,
Gwendolyn."

The murder board bristled with pins and red yarn slicing across states.

"Every postmark is from a different state." Wally tapped a pin near the coast. "Whoever sent these has traveled more than a long-distance trucker."

"That's one explanation." Tammy crossed her arms.

Olivia traced the yarn's path with her eyes. "Or they're running from something."

"Or someone." Wally stepped back from the board.

Olivia turned to face the group. "What did we learn?"

"It's the same story over and over." Xander gestured to the letters. "Except from a different location."

Olivia spread the scanned letters across the back room's table. "Each one's addressed to Jeremiah and signed by Gwendolyn. Every letter anchors itself to winter and Christmas, circles back to a cemetery, and mentions the stories he used to tell."

A pattern. Always a pattern when people were hiding something.

"She talks about leaving suddenly, regretting it, says she can't tell the full truth, and keeps moving from place to place." Mrs. T set down her teacup. "The pattern's steady: distance, longing, secrecy, and always an object which she refers to in ways such as a memento, our lifeline, and something that never leaves her."

"If the names are a cover," Olivia said, "the letters might be in code too."

"Like a cipher?" Tammy picked up one of the pages.

"Oh, that is brilliant," said Mrs. T.

Olivia divided up the letters. "We read them again. We test for patterns. Reused lines, odd capitalization, acrostics, page margins, anything that spells a breadcrumb."

The bookstore bell jingled.

Olivia crossed into the front room.

Mr. Taylor, the postmaster, stood in the doorway with his mailbag slung over one shoulder. He studied the new glass. "I heard about your window. You'll want to keep watch, Miss Huddlestone. Town's not as trustworthy as it used to be. My back room window's always cracked open. Never been an issue, but this morning the sill looked wiped clean, and my kettle was turned the wrong way. Only I touch that kettle."

Olivia's stomach dipped. *Does he know it was us? No. He can't.*

"M-Margaret probably cleaned up and bumped the kettle on the way out. She sometimes cleans after you've left, doesn't she?"

His jaw tightened. "Margaret knows better than to be in there alone at this time of year. I almost called the sheriff, but nothing was missing, so I let it be. Still, I could have."

Olivia manufactured something she hoped passed for casual. "I'm sure it was nothing."

"Maybe." His gaze lingered a beat too long. Then he tipped his cap. "I'll be keeping that window shut from now on."

She held her breath until the door closed behind him. *He knows.*

She lingered by the window, scanning the street, then returned to the back room.

Tammy flipped through her notes. "I've checked for codes—first letters, paragraphs, punctuation, repeated words, anything out of place. Nothing. No secret phrases or hidden strings. If there's a code, it's something known only to them."

Across the table, Xander adjusted his laptop screen. "The database I created agrees. There's only one oddity. Every December, a letter was mailed before Christmas except one. The first one came after."

1995. The year everything shifted.

Xander tapped a few keys. "I pulled the Willow Crafters' anecdotes, the case file, and a couple of online resources, then cross-checked. The timeline says: Archie's grandfather died on 15 July 1995, the blizzard hit on 21 December. In the early hours of 22 December, Archie was found in the cemetery. On the same day, his mom reported the necklace missing, the tree lighting happened, and Georgina learned the inn family was gone. The first letter is postmarked 27 December."

Olivia added the timeline to the board.

Wally pushed back from the table, his chair scraping against the floor. "Sounds like a good place to stop for tonight."

Mrs. T gathered her shawl. "Don't forget about tomorrow. Six a.m. sharp at the State Park entrance or Marjorie will be furious."

CHAPTER 12

Lockie meowed and lifted one frozen paw, then another, in clear protest.

"I know." Tammy dug through her pocket for her gloves. "But you insisted on coming."

She scanned the square. Olivia strode toward her.

"Morning!" Olivia's enthusiasm oozed out. "Ready to string up enough lights to be seen from space?"

Tammy fell into step beside her. "As ready as I'll ever be. Though I'm still not sure how I let you talk me into this."

Snow crunched beneath their boots. The towering pines loomed overhead, their frost-laden needles catching the early light. She tugged her scarf tighter. The northern cold seeped into her bones, so different from what she'd grown up with.

"The team's all here." Wally shattered the stillness.

Tammy grinned. The retired detective stood near a pile of tangled lights. Mrs. T issued directions beside him.

"Wouldn't miss it." Tammy approached the group. "Though I might need a gallon of coffee to function."

"You and me both." Xander trudged up behind them, looking like he'd rather be anywhere else.

Olivia reached out and ruffled his hair. "Come on, kiddo. Where's your Christmas spirit?"

Xander ducked away and shot her a glare. "Sleeping."

Mrs. T clucked her tongue. "Now, now. There's nothing normal about sleeping through a beautiful morning."

Tammy pressed her lips together. The kid wanted to argue. His jaw twitched, but even he couldn't resist Mrs. T's grandmotherly charm.

"Gather round, everyone!" Marjorie sliced through the chatter. She stood atop a makeshift platform, silver hair coiffed to perfection despite the early hour. "We have a tight schedule to keep if we want these lights strung before nightfall."

They joined the huddle.

Wally jerked his chin toward the refreshment table. "I'll grab us a round. This could be a long one with Marjorie at the helm."

"You think she sleeps in those pearls?" Xander whispered.

Olivia stifled a snort.

"Do try to remember Marjorie and I are friends, dears." Mrs. T's tone held gentle reproach.

Wally returned with steaming cups. Marjorie doled out assignments with drill sergeant authority. Tammy sipped the scalding liquid and let it revive her from within. Focus on the task at hand. The mystery can wait.

The work began. Tammy hauled strings of lights, climbed ladders, and wound cables around branches. Even Xander's grumbling faded as the sky lightened, painting the snow in soft pinks and golds.

She paused and took in the newly illuminated stretch. This was the path Wally had described, where the town ring their collection of bells.

"You know..." Mrs. T stopped and surveyed their progress. "I do believe this might be our best display yet."

The corner of Wally's mouth quirked up. "It's certainly something. Though I still say we should have gone with my idea for the animatronic reindeer."

A collective groan rose from the group.

"For the last time, Wally." Olivia planted her hands on her hips. "We are not terrorizing small children with your robo-deer army."

Tammy snickered.

The temperature dropped another degree as Marjorie's command cut through the frost.

"No, no, no! The silver tinsel goes on the evergreens, not the birches. Honestly, do I have to spell everything out?"

Marjorie marched through the volunteers, clipboard clutched to her chest. Tammy caught Olivia's eye.

Olivia leaned close. "I swear, she runs this event like a military operation."

Marjorie zeroed in on a hapless volunteer who struggled with a string of lights.

"Oh dear." Mrs. T winced. "That poor boy's about to get an earful."

"Young man, those lights are meant to sparkle, not strangle the tree!" Marjorie's words carried across the clearing.

Xander laughed. "Ten bucks says she makes him cry."

Olivia elbowed him. "That's terrible. True, but terrible."

At least Marjorie keeps things interesting. Tammy grabbed another bundle of lights.

Olivia hoisted a tangled mass over her shoulder and trudged through the snow. Her breath came out in frosty clouds.

"Careful, Liv!" Tammy called.

"I think I can handle a few strands of..." Olivia's foot caught on something hidden under a drift. She stumbled. The lights flew from her grasp as she pitched forward.

"Olivia!" Mrs. T's alarmed cry rang out.

"Liv! Are you okay?" Tammy rushed over.

Olivia's head popped up, snow dusting her auburn hair. She spat out a mouthful of powder. Her glasses sat crooked on her nose. "Well, that was graceful. I think I found a new way to make snow angels. Face first!"

Tammy extended her hand. "What did you trip over?"

"I don't know. A log?" She turned and peered at the white-capped lump behind her. "Let's see what..."

She brushed aside the drift. A pale, lifeless hand emerged.

Olivia scrambled backward. Color drained from her face. "Oh biscuits. That's... not a log."

"Wally!" Tammy's voice cracked. "Get over here!"

The others materialized in seconds. Wally crouched down and examined the find.

"This just became a crime scene."

"Body!" Olivia's shriek pierced the morning stillness. "There's a body!"

Chapter 13

Chaos detonated.

Volunteers screamed. Ladders crashed against the trail. A crate of spare bulbs toppled and shattered across the white.

"Back up! Give us room!" Wally thrust an arm out to shield the body as people lurched and stumbled.

Tammy stood rooted to the spot.

This can't be happening. Not again.

Someone clipped her shoulder. A string of lights skittered past her boots.

"I know him!" Olivia swept snow from the body's face. "He helped Mr. Applewood lift the nutcracker after it fell!"

"You sure?" Wally scanned the ground around them.

"Yes!" The word tore from Olivia's throat. "Same face. Same coat!"

"Everyone, please remain calm!" Marjorie's command cut through the screaming. She strode toward the center of the group, spine straight, eyes hard as flint. "All volunteers return to the parking lot and await further instructions."

The volunteers scattered despite their murmuring.

Marjorie approached. Her mouth thinned to a bloodless line. "You'd think they'd never seen a dead body before. Amateurs."

Tammy shot a glance at the woman. *Was that a wink?*

"I trust you'll handle this situation with discretion." Marjorie made a slow circuit of their faces. "The last thing we need is wild speculation and rumors spreading through town."

"We'll do our best to keep things contained until the sheriff arrives." Wally's jaw set.

Marjorie's attention drifted toward the body. She went still. Her head tilted. Her mouth opened, then closed. She blinked twice, gaze flicking from the man's face to his coat and back. Her fingers twitched at her side.

Tammy waited for her to speak, but the older woman sealed her lips and stepped back.

"What should we do?" Tammy pulled her coat tighter.

Wally knelt beside the body, his movements precise and practiced. "We need to gather as much evidence as we can before the sheriff shoos us away. Rule number one: we look, but we don't touch. Anything we spot, we document."

He pulled out his phone and gestured for them to do the same. "Use your cameras, and keep your distance."

Tammy raised her phone. *Every rule sounded straightforward until you were standing in front of a real body.* Fiction never prepared her for how quiet death felt.

Wally sidestepped around the scene. "See how I'm avoiding the obvious footprints? We don't want to add to the confusion."

He reached into his coat and tugged on a pair of latex gloves. "I always carry a set. Old habits die hard."

Xander raised an eyebrow. "And here I thought you'd retired."

Wally's lips quirked. "You never know when you might need them."

Xander lowered his camera. "What, in case you stumble across a crime scene while grocery shopping?"

"Do you remember our history?" Wally's tone carried amusement beneath the gruffness.

"Guess I'll keep my camera handy at Mrs. Hubbard's Cupboard, then."

"Do that." Wally's expression remained dry. "Now capture every angle."

As Tammy snapped photos, the man in front of her transformed. Gone was the affable retiree; in his place stood a seasoned investigator.

"Xander," Wally continued, "I know you're not fond of this sort of thing."

Xander gulped. "R-right. Pretend it's a really macabre fashion shoot."

Mrs. T tutted. "Oh, for heaven's sake. It's just a body, dear. Nothing to lose your lunch over."

"I don't know how you all do it." Xander's camera trembled in his grip. "Me, no matter how many bodies we come across, I will never get used to it."

Where's Lockie?

As if summoned, her cat emerged from a nearby bush, dragging a knitted scarf in his mouth.

"Lockie, no!" Tammy lunged for the item. "Drop it, you furry felon!"

Wally chuckled. "We've got ourselves a four-pawed accomplice. Make sure he doesn't contaminate any more evidence."

"This is like one of your books, Tammy?" Mrs. T said. "Though I doubt you've written a scene where a feline compromises a clue."

Lockie gave an indignant mrrp from his perch on a nearby log.

"Oh hush, you." Tammy shot him a look. "And no, Mrs. T, I can't say I have."

Lockie trotted a few paces away, his tail flicking. He gave a sharp meow and pawed at a particular spot.

"What's he doing now?"

Mrs. T peered over. "He's found something far less festive than scarves."

Tammy hurried over and brushed aside the powder near where Lockie had been digging. The color stopped her.

"Wally…" Her throat constricted, forcing the words through a narrowed passage. "Is that what I think it is?"

He lowered himself onto one knee. His Adam's apple bobbed. "Yes. It's seeped into the snow and frozen in layers, creating this red marbled effect."

Tammy's saliva turned metallic. Her molars clenched. "What does that mean?"

Wally straightened, his eyes meeting hers. "It suggests the body has been here overnight."

The victim had lain there, alone in the cold. Tammy's fingers dug into her coat sleeves.

Olivia gasped. "So he wasn't killed this morning?"

"No," Wally confirmed. "This gives us a timeline."

The killer had time to leave town.

Lockie trotted up beside Tammy and gave a soft, approving chirp, his tail flicking. "You always know where to look, don't you?"

He blinked slowly.

Xander stood a little apart, his camera drooping at his side, his face drained of color. Tammy nudged Olivia and bobbed her head in his direction.

"Xander," Olivia said softly. "Come here for a second."

He jerked his head up and stepped closer. "Did I do something wrong?"

Olivia rested a steady hand on his arm. "No. I wanted to check on you."

"I'm okay." His words wavered. "I want to help."

"You are helping." Olivia's grip tightened briefly. "Just remember to take care of yourself too. It's okay to feel rattled."

He blinked hard, then drew a deep breath and straightened his shoulders. "I won't let you down."

Olivia moved a few paces to the left and brushed aside a light drift. "Hold on. Something shiny." She teased a scrap from the crusted surface. "A candy wrapper."

"Photos first. Do not touch." Wally's command rang across the clearing.

Olivia set the wrapper back where it had been. "Right. Evidence etiquette." She raised her phone and took several shots from different angles. "This is from Sugarplum Confectionery. Their packaging always looks good enough to eat."

Mrs. T cocked her head. "The store in Oaktown?"

"Whoever dropped this has a sweet tooth and has been to Oaktown." Olivia studied the wrapper.

"We've all been to Oaktown," Xander said.

"True." Olivia's lips curved. "The flavor of this kind of clue depends entirely on who had the first bite. Victim or killer?"

The group groaned, but Olivia grinned.

Wally inspected the wrapper from a distance. "Could be a lead, could be noise. Either way, it doesn't belong out here."

Tammy stared at the scrap of foil glinting against the white. *Was someone eating candy while a man lay dead in the snow?*

Lockie hovered at her boots. "What have we gotten ourselves into this time, buddy?" She gave him a scratch under the chin.

"What about smell?" Mrs. T piped up. "I swear I caught a whiff of peppermint earlier."

"Your nose helped once before with the honey, remember?" said Olivia.

"Everything's important until it's not." Wally appraised the wrapper. "Note it down, but do not go sniffing around. We leave that to the professionals."

Did Wally make a joke?

"You'd think everyone in Michigan has discovered mint flavoring this week." Mrs. T waved off the scent. "It's everywhere."

"Doesn't this all seem a bit convenient?" Tammy refocused. "A body showing up right when we're deep in the Beaumont mystery?"

Wally looked at her. "Now you're in detective mode. But remember, correlation does not always mean causation."

"In my books, it does," Tammy said.

"Hold on." Olivia dropped to a knee. "Those marks aren't random."

"What do you see?" asked Wally.

"It isn't a snow angel gone wrong." Olivia's humor thinned. "Look at the pattern. The grooves cut deeper under the dusting."

Tammy squinted. Scuffs and gouges blurred across the surface, a tangle that didn't belong in the calm drift.

Wally went down into a careful squat without crossing the boundary. "Those marks suggest a struggle. Our victim didn't go down easy."

"Our town's secrets are a bubbling pot of mulled wine left too long on the stove," Olivia said.

Tammy's foot kicked something solid. "Hey, what's this?" She knelt. Lockie sat by her. "It's a wallet."

The world narrowed to the small leather square. "Should we?"

Wally stepped forward. "We need to know who he is. But no one touches it without gloves."

He eased the wallet free, his movements careful and deliberate. Inside, a driver's license and a few business cards lay neatly tucked.

"James Morton," Wally read aloud. "A private investigator from Chicago."

"He looks like the man Henry met at the cemetery," Tammy said.

Olivia's glasses slid down her nose as she stared. "So Thomas was right."

Tammy exhaled. "If he was chasing the necklace, he might've uncovered something that led to this."

Wally's expression darkened. "If Morton was killed for getting close to the truth, and if the killer finds out about us—"

Tammy met his gaze. "We need to be a step ahead."

She stood, brushing powder from her knees. The others spread out and scanned the nearby brush.

A glint of color snagged Tammy's attention. "Mrs. T, come take a look at this." She pointed to a low branch near a silver birch.

Mrs. T hurried over and bent close. "Oh my. This is not any old thread. That is hand-dyed alpaca blended with silk, I'd wager. The sheen gives it away."

Tammy tilted her head. "You can tell that from one strand?"

"When you've been knitting as many winters as I have, you learn to tell the difference between cheap acrylic and art." She straightened. "It might be the Winter Solstice colorway, but I'll need to confirm."

She took a photo and tapped out a message. "Della Mae keeps every yarn catalog she's ever received."

By the time Wally finished inspecting the ground beneath the branch, Mrs. T's phone chimed. She read the reply and gave a satisfied nod. "Confirmed. Winter Solstice, cranberry and gold. Sold mostly online and in a handful of artisan markets each year." She looked toward town. "And this winter, the maker has a stall at our Christmas market."

Tammy folded her arms, the cold biting through her sleeves. "It's a lead, all right. But we don't know if it ties to the victim or the killer." *Or a red herring.*

Wally stood. "Either way, we'll let the sheriff's team decide. We make sure they find it."

He paused. "There's something in his hand."

Tammy stepped closer. A glossy corner of paper peeked out, creased and edged with frost.

"Photo first." He took a close shot of the hand.

"Is that a photograph?" asked Olivia.

Wally eased the edge free, lifting it without disturbing the rest. He brushed away a veil of snow, and the faint image sharpened.

Olivia's breath caught. "That's the Beaumont ruby necklace."

Xander moved in, camera raised. "It can't be."

The unmistakable crimson sparkle of the jewels blazed against a pale throat.

"This was taken much later than 1995," Tammy scrutinized the details. "The woman in the background is holding a flip phone."

No one spoke. The winter wind whistled through the trees.

Xander captured a few careful shots before Wally slid the photo back into the victim's hand. "We'll let the sheriff's team collect it properly."

Olivia crossed her arms. "If word gets out that the necklace might've resurfaced—"

"The whole town will lose its mind," Mrs. T finished.

Wally glanced around at each of them in turn. "Then it stays between us."

A twig snapped.

CHAPTER 14

Sheriff Stanton strode toward them, Lamby padding a step ahead, nose low, ears flicking at every sound. Deputy Brown followed close behind, hand resting on his holster.

Tammy shifted her weight.

Stanton stopped in front of the group. "Morning. *You all* discovered the body?"

He doesn't believe this is a coincidence.

Wally stepped forward, spine straight. "That's right. We were setting up for the light show when Olivia stumbled upon him."

The sheriff scanned the team, lingering for a beat on each face. "I hope you all aren't getting ideas about playing detective on this one. Leave the investigating to us professionals."

Heat flared in Tammy's chest. Her mouth opened.

Wally's head turned a fraction.

She shut it.

"Of course," Wally said. "We wouldn't dream of interfering."

Stanton grunted. "Secure the scene."

Brown moved off with his notepad.

"I don't want anyone else trampling through here."

Lamby drifted to the edge of the churned path, pacing a slow circle outside the obvious footprints. He sneezed twice, sharp and papery.

Stanton's head whipped toward his dog before he faced the group once more. "I'll need statements from each of you."

The sheriff crossed to the body, shoulders squared, jaw set. Tammy huddled closer to the others. "So much for keeping our theories quiet. He thinks we're up to something."

"That's better than being suspects," Xander said.

Wally tracked Stanton's movements. "Once we give our statements, we'll step back. We're not giving the killer any help by tiptoeing into an obstruction charge."

Xander fidgeted. "What's our next move?"

Wally dropped his volume to barely audible. "Xander, dig into Morton's background."

Tammy kept one ear on Wally and the other on the officers.

Stanton's command carried over the brittle wind. "What have we got?"

The deputy crouched near the body. "Victim is James Morton, Chicago address. Wallet found nearby with ID but no cash."

Stanton scanned the scene. "Robbery gone wrong. Pockets turned out, no phone. Likely a drifter passing through."

Look at his hand.

"Signs of a struggle," Brown said.

Stanton gestured toward the perimeter. "Disturbed snow. Broken branches. He fought and lost. Simple."

Tammy's fingernails bit into her palms. The marbling. The specialty candy wrapper. The strand of yarn. The photo. None of it was simple.

Her lower lip disappeared between her teeth.

Lamby veered toward them and froze. From Tammy's boots, Lockie rose to full bottle-brush, ears flat, a low hiss threaded with steam. The dog inclined his head, perfectly still. Two pet detectives sharing one patch. For three heartbeats, nobody moved.

"Ea-sy." Tammy scooped Lockie up. His eyes remained pinned on the dog, pupils dilated.

"Time to clear out, folks." Sheriff Stanton waved them away. "We'll take it from here."

Wally cleared his throat. "Of course, Sheriff. We understand."

But Tammy caught the slight arch of his eyebrow, a silent signal to the group. *Step back physically. Think forward.*

Stanton whistled. Lamby broke the stare and curved around the group with exaggerated manners, skirting the main footprints. He eased toward the victim's side, nose hovering over the contracted hand, then lifted one paw and looked up at Stanton.

Tammy peeked over her shoulder as they turned to go. The sheriff bent to inspect what Lamby was alerting him to.

After a handful of steps, Stanton boomed, "Hold it."

Tammy spun around. The sheriff straightened with the photograph pinched between his gloved fingers.

"Let's try this again."

The team exchanged glances. Wally exhaled slowly, the faintest shake of his head telling them to stay quiet.

Stanton moved from face to face, then down to the image. "What haven't you told me?"

He turned to Wally. "That's the necklace from the case file I gave you?"

Wally kept his face calm, but the muscle at the corner of his jaw jumped. "Looks that way."

"Care to explain how our murder victim ended up holding evidence from a thirty-year-old theft you just happened to take an interest in?"

Tammy's tongue stuck to the roof of her mouth.

Wally's breath steamed silver. "Our cold case got warmer."

Stanton's stare didn't waver. "Then I suggest you start talking."

Chapter 15

The bell jangled as they filed into Bookworm Haven, boots leaving wet trails across the mat. Heat poured from the radiators. Lockie sprang from Tammy's bag, shook himself, and bolted toward the back room's hidden entrance.

Olivia threw the deadbolt. "I need caffeine before my soul mutinies."

"Make it a round." Wally pulled off his coat. "We've got evidence to analyze."

They followed Lockie to their secret lair.

Xander set his phone on the table. "All photos backed up. The wrapper, yarn, scuffs, wallet. The photo of the photo."

They gathered around. The shock had drained, but the thrill remained: a Chicago PI dead in the snow and a photo of a necklace that shouldn't exist.

Wally drummed his fingers. "Ground rule. No speculation outside this room. Stanton has the scene. We chase public threads such as volunteers, markets, Oaktown."

Mrs. T unwound her scarf and sank into her chair. "One step at a time, dears."

"Okay." Tammy pulled herself into focus. "Tasks."

Olivia held up a finger. "I'm claiming the candy wrapper. I know the owner, Nora." She tapped at her phone. "Their store is closed today."

"Don't forget the scent. Could be gum, oil, or confection." Mrs. T's knitting had already materialized in her hands like a conjuring trick.

"Sugarplum Confectionery has a peppermint bark," Olivia said. "But the wrapper we found isn't the correct size for that."

Mrs. T's needles clicked. "We can talk to the Winter Solstice yarn artisan when they arrive in town."

"Maybe they left it when they killed Morton," said Olivia.

"No jumping to conclusions. I own a shawl made in Winter Solstice. Does that make me a suspect?"

Mrs. T didn't give anyone time to answer. "Here it is." She passed around her phone. "I want you all to be familiar with the colorway. Xander, print it and put it on the board, please."

Olivia poured the fresh coffee and distributed hot mugs.

Xander went to the printer and placed a brightly colored picture on the board.

"Wow." Tammy tilted her head. "No way I'd miss anyone wearing something in that color."

Xander pulled his laptop closer. "I'll work on the photo. Facial recognition programs will be tricky since it's a photo of a photo, but I'll try."

"Could the necklace be a forgery?" Olivia asked.

"Let's work on the assumption it is the real thing." Wally set down his pen. "Given it was found in the hand of a deceased PI who's been hired to find it."

Xander concentrated on his screen. "I've used the Beaumont website photos to run the ruby through object-recognition software after getting the idea from those bonkers internet search results thanks to the shared town Wi-Fi. It hasn't turned up anything yet. A Chicago PI might have had access to a better program than I can make and found the photo that way."

"Are there any cameras in that part of the park?" Olivia asked. "We fundraised for more after the bear incident."

"They are located off the trails. Animals generally avoid humans." Xander shrugged. "And I doubt anyone saw anything. Park Ranger Dad didn't get any call-outs last night. I didn't hear the phone, but I heard him snoring as I left."

Wally tapped his mug. "At least Stanton's 'robbery gone wrong' has been debunked. That photo suggests the necklace resurfaced, and that could be motive for murder."

Lockie chirped from his perch. Tammy reached up and scratched his chin. "Lockie agrees."

Wally stood and started to pace. "What do we know about this James Morton?"

"I'm on his website." Tammy scrolled. "He specialized in cold cases involving missing persons and art thefts."

Olivia's head snapped up. "So a necklace assumed stolen by a missing family is right in his specialty."

"He's known for using unconventional methods, whatever that means."

"Like meeting a source in a state park at night?" said Mrs. T.

Tammy's pen hovered above her notebook. "Morton could've arranged to authenticate it or negotiate its return." She paused. "Unless anyone has any other ideas, we assume the family from the inn has the necklace, and Henry Beaumont hired Morton to find it and them."

Wally stopped pacing. "Archie sounded genuine when he said he never wanted to see it again."

"So we hone in on Henry," said Olivia.

"What about the letters?" Tammy set down her pen. "Are they connected?"

Wally resumed his seat. "Maybe they are, and maybe not. The murder comes first. If they're connected, and we're lucky we might solve the letters along the way."

PING

Xander's legs bounced. "My object-recognition software has a hit!"

"For the necklace?" asked Olivia.

"It's the same photo Morton had. He must have found it the same way." He turned his laptop to face the others. "It's from an art gallery opening in Florida in 2004 and is on their website. Morton has cropped and enlarged the photo. It was a wide event shot, the kind no one poses for or even notices being taken."

"Can we get a copy of the original to help with facial recognition?" asked Wally.

Xander wrote down a number and passed it to Wally. "You call them and ask in your best sheriff voice."

Wally didn't hesitate. He dialed and asked.

"I'm sorry. Did you say someone else asked for the same photo two weeks ago?"

The PI was way ahead of them.

Wally hung up. "He's sending us a copy. Now we know how Morton got it."

"I'm all set up for a facial recognition trace as soon as it comes through," said Xander.

Mrs. T's phone vibrated with the persistence of a hyperactive squirrel, practically shimmying across the table. She snatched it up. "The Knotty but Nice group chat is on fire." She scrolled ferociously. "Half the town's already heard about the body."

"With any luck, they'll have it solved before Stanton even dusts for prints," said Wally.

"Mock if you must, but those ladies hear everything. Rumor runs fast. Facts sometimes hitch a ride."

Tammy wrapped her hands around her near empty mug. The group's collective chatter had a way of making her head buzz. Too many maybes, clouds, and what-ifs. She needed air.

She pushed back her chair. "I'm going outside. If we want a read on Henry, he's probably in the square, wrangling the market volunteers and vendors."

Lockie launched from his perch and followed her out.

CHAPTER 16

While Tammy headed into the cold, gossip traveled faster than the frost via the Knotty but Nice group text.

Betty: I still can't believe there was a body found at the light walk setup. It's dreadful. But also sort of thrilling. It's straight out of a Christmas mystery novel!

Marjorie: It's not a novel, Betty. It's real life, and it's thrown my entire event schedule into chaos.

Beatrice: Oh, is the light show canceled? I just finished knitting my snowflake hat for opening night.

Marjorie: Of course it's not canceled. We'll reroute around the scene. The lights must go on.

Della Mae: Georgina said the man wasn't staying at the Inn, which is odd since he wasn't a local and there's nowhere else to stay in town. Makes you wonder where he was sleeping.

Betty: Maybe with a sweetheart!

Marjorie: Don't be absurd. I saw him four days ago near the Beaumont estate talking with the gardener, if you can call that mumbling man a gardener.

That puts him in town before he helped Olivia with the nutcracker.

Hazel: You didn't mention this earlier. Are you sure?

Marjorie: I didn't immediately place him. And I'm positive of the timing because it was during my weekly constitutional walk along Founder's Row. I always take it to monitor any breaches of town planning in the heritage district.

Della Mae: You mean you were snooping again.

Marjorie: Civic vigilance. There's a difference.

Betty: Maybe he was admiring the gardens. Or searching for buried treasure!

Marjorie: He wasn't admiring begonias. They seemed deep in discussion. I heard him say "she," "Ruby," and something about a chair.

Hazel paused, her fingers hovering over the keys.

Beatrice: Ruby who? Do we know her?

Betty: Maybe she was his lost love! She begged him to meet her under the Christmas lights, but fate intervened!

Marjorie: Betty, not everything is a romance novel.

Hazel: Still, it's curious. A stranger in town, not staying at the Inn, seen at the Beaumont estate, and now maybe talking about the ruby necklace.

Marjorie: Oh, well done. Of course that's what it was.

Della Mae: The whole thing gives me chills. Georgina says the guests are all gossiping, and George is grumbling that crime scenes don't boost tourism.

Beatrice: Poor man. And poor Marjorie.

Marjorie: Willowcroft deserves its light show. We'll add more illumination. We can't have dark corners now, can we?

Betty: Oooh, poetic! Justice by fairy lights!

Marjorie: Practical, not poetic.

Hazel: Either way, it's very Willowcroft of you.

CHAPTER 17

A gust sliced through the square and stole Tammy's breath.

She yanked her scarf higher. Lockie trotted beside her, tail twitching, nose lifted into the wind. A low chuff escaped his throat. Part sneeze, part complaint.

The Christmas market preparations hummed at half volume around her. Workers' conversations dropped to murmurs. Hammers struck wood in uncertain rhythms.

A disheveled figure gestured weakly at a cluster of confused vendors across the cobblestones. Henry Beaumont.

Time to poke the bear.

Lockie padded ahead.

The man who had supposedly obsessed over stall placement last year now wore his jacket buttoned askew. His salt-and-pepper hair jutted at angles that defied gravity. Smudges darkened the skin beneath his eyes.

"Mr. Beaumont!" Tammy raised her hand. "How's the setup going?"

He jerked, grabbed for his phone in his pocket, then shoved it deeper. "Oh, Miss Rumbelow. It's fine. Everything's fine."

"Really?" Tammy let her attention drift to a sagging banner. The crooked letters proclaimed *Merry Chrismas!*

Lockie pawed at the fallen corner as if pointing out the mistake.

Henry noticed the sign and flinched. "Ah, well. We'll add a 't' later. Probably."

A vendor setting up leaned toward her neighbor. "Last year he made us measure the distance between stands with a ruler."

The man had never been this discombobulated in public view. She stepped closer. "Need a coffee?"

"I'm fine!" The snap came sharp, then crumpled. "Sorry. Bad night."

Am I talking to the killer? Maybe I shouldn't have come on my own.

Meow.

Right, I'm not alone.

Henry's pocket vibrated. He yanked the phone out, scanned the screen, and jammed it back without responding.

Tammy kept at him. "Tell me about the gingerbread house competition. Is that new?"

Henry's gaze darted from her face to his coat pocket. "Oh, yes. Gingerbread. Very festive."

A knot of workers huddled three stalls down cast glances in Henry's direction. One said, "I've never seen him this way. Do you think it has something to do with—"

Henry's head whipped toward them. Lockie's fur rippled along his spine. Tammy committed the vendor's words to memory, filing them next to the crooked banner and Henry's trembling hands.

She kept her tone light. "Your family started this market, right? That's quite a legacy to maintain."

He scrubbed a hand through his tousled hair, making it worse. "You'd think I'd have it down by now."

His pocket thrummed. He pulled the phone free, stared at the screen, turned three shades paler, then killed the call and gripped the device tight.

"Trouble?"

His head jerked up. His pupils dilated. A muscle jumped in his jaw. His empty hand found his collar and tugged. "What? No. Spam calls."

He shifted his weight, blocking her view of the screen. Lockie padded forward, sniffed near Henry's boots, and gave a short, disapproving mrrow. Tammy scooped him up.

A volunteer called out, "Hey, Henry, where do you want the mistletoe arch?"

Henry blinked at him. "The... oh, right. Um, wherever."

The volunteer's mouth fell open. "'Wherever'? But last year you made us move it six times!"

His spine bent. The meticulous market maestro the town whispered about had vanished.

"Henry." Tammy kept her voice soft. "If something's wrong I can help with—"

"Nothing's wrong!" He winced. Color crept up his neck. He couldn't face her. "I need some space."

He hurried away, the phone still clutched in his fist. Lockie fixed on the retreating figure, tail tip twitching.

Tammy glanced around the square. The whispers multiplied. Concerned expressions followed Henry's retreat. Whatever had him on edge, others had picked up on it too.

She followed at a distance, weaving through half-assembled stalls. Henry's shoulders hunched tighter with each step.

He whirled, angling toward a crooked food stand. "For heaven's sake!" The bark startled a freckle-faced girl arranging displays. "Can't you see that's completely lopsided?"

The girl jolted. "I'm sorry, Mr. Beaumont. I'll fix it right away."

Henry's hand shook as it rose to his ear. "No, I... you got us into this... Stop."

He turned away. Tammy edged closer, pretending to admire pottery being laid out at a stall. Lockie hopped onto a crate beside her, crouched low, and flicked his tail in time with Henry's rising agitation.

Henry's mutter barely reached her ears. "What a waste of time. Should've left it alone."

Left what alone? The necklace? The PI? Lockie inclined his head toward the sheriff's office across the square, as if following Henry's line of sight.

This went beyond holiday stress.

He ended the call.

She cleared her throat and painted on her brightest face. "Mr. Beaumont? I'd love to learn about the market traditions. Being new in town and all."

Henry's head snapped up. He launched into a rehearsed speech. "The Willowcroft Christmas Market has been a cornerstone of our community for over a century. My great-grandfather started the tradition back in—"

He cut himself off. His face tightened. He shoved both still-quivering hands into his pockets.

"Your family must be so proud of that legacy."

Henry's jaw clenched. "Yes, well, traditions change, don't they?"

"I've heard whispers about a special family heirloom. A necklace, I think? Is that part of the market's history too?"

His face contorted. "Where did you hear about that?" He took a step toward her, then stopped short, fists tightening at his sides. "It's none of your business! You outsiders, always poking around where you don't belong!"

Lockie hissed at him.

Tammy stepped back. "I didn't mean to pry—"

"Just stay out of it!"

Lockie pressed close to her boot, back arched, tail puffed.

A loud crash split the air behind them. A market hut collapsed, its wooden frame splintered across the cobblestones.

Henry whirled. A vein pulsed at his temple.

"For goodness' sake!" He stomped toward the wreckage. Tammy followed, biting her lip. Lockie padded beside her.

Henry seized the frame and yanked it upright. His muscles strained against the stubborn wood. "Absolutely useless." The mutter spilled out. "Can't get decent hired help anymore. Can't even set up a simple stand without—"

He blinked rapidly. "I didn't mean... that is to say..."

Hired help? The market setup ran on volunteers and stallholders.

"Mr. Beaumont." She chose each word with care. "This must be exhausting. Have you had any time off recently?"

Henry's shoulders curved inward. His hands hung loose at his sides. Then he straightened.

"I'm fine. It's been a demanding week."

Tammy took the plunge. "I hope you don't mind me asking, but where were you last night? You know, before the body in the state park was found?"

His face drained to gray. His eyes tracked the path to the corner twice. "I-I have to go. Urgent business. Just remembered."

"But—"

"Good day, Ms. Rumbelow!"

He sprinted across the square.

Tammy hugged herself against the chill.

She ran through the evidence: the phone calls he wouldn't answer, and the one he did, the "hired help" slip, his reaction to the necklace question, no alibi given but a late night, the sprint away in the opposite direction of the sheriff's building.

Henry Beaumont knew something about Morton's death. The question was whether guilt drove him or fear.

As he vanished around the corner, a flicker of movement pulled Tammy's attention. Lockie sat at her boot, tail wrapped neatly, watching the same direction with mild feline interest.

Margaret Taylor stood near a stall, her coat done up tight, focus flicking from Tammy to the empty lane Henry had taken. She had seen the whole thing.

Time to see what the postmaster's wife knew.

Tammy pasted on her most disarming smile and crossed the cobbles, mindful of the ice without her snowshoes. Lockie padded after her, his paw prints making small crescents beside hers.

"Mrs. Taylor, lovely to see you. How are you?"

Margaret's smile stretched. "Oh, Tammy dear, I'm just peachy. I caught your spirited conversation with Henry. Everything all right?"

Tammy shrugged, aiming for nonchalance. "Just a misunderstanding, I'm sure. You know how holiday stress can get to people."

Lockie gave a soft chuff, as if agreeing that humans become strange at Christmas.

"Mm, indeed," Margaret said, her tone syrupy with sympathy that didn't quite ring true. "Though I must say, there's been a bit of... tension in town lately."

Tammy's eyebrows shot up. "The body of an out-of-towner was found in the state park, Mrs. Taylor."

Margaret leaned in, her gloved hand suddenly clamping Tammy's forearm with surprising strength. Peppermint and sugar laced her breath. "My husband told you about the letters." She checked the air around them. "Are you... looking into them?"

Keep calm. She doesn't know.

"He mentioned them, but it's a federal offense to open them, even for the postmaster, since we don't have an official Dead Letter Office. So there's nothing to investigate."

Margaret flinched, a hiccup of a laugh escaping. "Federal offense. My stars. Who would risk that?" Her hand went to her hair, trembling as she fussed with a curl. "As if anyone would actually... well. Nonsense."

Tammy dipped her chin as if satisfied, though she didn't miss the color high on Margaret's cheeks. If anyone in Willowcroft had both the proximity and the privacy to meddle with undeliverable mail, it was the postmaster's wife.

Margaret cleared her throat. "You're a sharp girl. You must have... picked up on things." Her words wobbled out before she gained composure. "We all care about this community. If something untoward is in the mix, we ought to see it sorted."

"Of course," Tammy said. "Community."

Margaret's grip softened, then returned with a quick pat. "Good. That's good." She reached into her handbag and produced a tin of peppermint bark that clinked against a thermos. "Have a good day now."

She moved off with careful steps, never once looking back.

Lockie sniffed at the minty scent in the air and sneezed delicately.

The thermos. The tremor. The way she'd steered the conversation straight to the letters and then sprinted away from it.

Margaret Taylor slid herself onto the suspect list with a neat little click.

CHAPTER 18

Olivia slipped out to see how the Christmas market was shaping up. She flung her coat over herself as she stood on the bookstore's stoop. Not much progress since yesterday. The most action came from a few volunteers arguing over whose ladder was taller.

"Miss Huddlestone!" Mrs. Peters charged at her, one hand clutching her hat, the other waving frantically. "Have you seen the Santa suit? It's vanished!"

Olivia blinked. "Did you check the Town Hall basement?"

"Twice," the woman groaned. "If we don't find it, the children will think Christmas is canceled."

Before Olivia could reassure her, her name carried across the square. Tammy crossed over, scarf flapping, Lockie at her side.

"Liv! I've had a very productive fresh air break."

Olivia braced herself. "Do tell."

Tammy leaned in. "Let's just say Henry Beaumont isn't the only one acting suspicious today. And his nerves? Wired tighter than one of Mrs. Peters' garlands."

Olivia stiffened. "You think he's hiding something?"

"Think it?" Tammy scoffed. "I'd bet my royalties on it." She linked arms with Olivia.

"Let's debrief in the warm. I need caffeine and plausible deniability."

They ducked into the store, the bell chiming as the door swung shut.

Tammy stopped at the counter. "Between Henry's cryptic muttering and Margaret Taylor shaking like a leaf, we've got two serious suspects for our Christmas mystery."

A burst of cold air rushed in through the reopened door. Mike entered, a dusting of snow glittering on his jacket.

"Hello." The calmness in his greeting made Olivia's pulse stutter. "Didn't mean to interrupt."

"You never interrupt," Olivia said too quickly, then wished she hadn't.

Tammy coughed into her hand. "I was leaving, actually. Cat emergency." She scooped up Lockie and shot Olivia a glare that said *good luck surviving your hormones.*

As the door closed behind her, Mike's smile softened. "I was checking on the market setup. Thought I'd stop by to make sure everything's secure here. With the crowd growing and, well..."

Olivia folded her arms, then unfolded them, then folded them again. "You think we need extra security?"

"My brother runs a security business in Oaktown. I help him out from time to time. I could sweep the place and offer suggestions?"

"Couldn't hurt."

He took in the store's layout, clipping a bookmark display with his elbow. Little cardboard cats scattered across the floor. "Oh—I'll just—" He bent down at the exact moment Olivia did. Their foreheads collided with a soft thunk.

"Ow!" they said in unison.

Mike pressed his palm to his forehead. "I've helped my brother with security, not... bookmarks."

"It's fine!" She shoved her glasses up so hard they went crooked. "That's... generous. Of you. The security thing."

"Want me to check things out now?" He gestured vaguely toward the door, nearly knocking over a mug of pens.

She nodded, maybe too eagerly. "Now's good."

Mike set his toolbox down and started inspecting the locks. "We could install a silent alarm," he said. "That alerts the sheriff's office instantly after hours."

"That sounds wonderful." Olivia's face flamed. "You're a real lifesaver, Mike. I could just eat you right—" She wanted to dissolve into the floorboards. "Eat that up. The idea! Not you. I don't eat people."

He turned, his ears turning bright red. "I'll take that as a compliment."

Olivia's fingers shredded the edge of a receipt.

"Maybe I'll stop by in a day or two," he said, voice cracking, "with more information."

"That's a delicious—I mean, delightful—I mean, fine idea."

Mike tripped over nothing as he moved to the door. "It's better to be careful. And keep the lights on after closing, just in case."

"I will." She followed him to the door. "Thanks. I'll see you out."

She reached for the doorknob. So did he. Their fingers tangled, her pinky somehow caught between his index and middle finger in an accidental hand-holding pretzel.

"Sorry!" they blurted, jumping apart. Mike banged his elbow on the door frame.

"Guess that's one way to test reflexes," he snorted. His hand flew to his mouth. He coughed, as if he could hide it.

Olivia's glasses slid down her nose. She pushed them up with such force that they nearly fell off her face. "Yes, well... excellent reaction time."

He backed toward the exit. "Soon then."

"Good." He gave a little wave that became an awkward salute. "I'll bring the alarm schematics… and maybe dessert. Unless you're full. From eating people."

He winced, turned too quickly, and walked straight into the closed door.

He made it through on the second try, leaving the tinkling bell and Olivia's own mortification echoing after him.

She collapsed behind the counter and fanned her cheeks with a magazine. "Smooth. Real smooth, Liv." Did it count as flirting if you referenced cannibalism?

Lockie slunk in as if to judge her. Olivia stuck out her tongue and was rewarded with a dismissive tail flick.

"Wait a minute—?" She looked toward the door. "You left with Tammy out the front. How did you get back in here?"

Lockie blinked once.

Either he was a shape-shifting specter, or Tammy had snuck in through the back.

Curiosity tugged harder than dignity. Olivia headed for the disguised door.

She eased it open and found two figures wobbling forward in unison. Mrs. T hugged her knitting bag to her chest; Tammy straightened, caught mid-eavesdrop.

"You were listening?"

"Monitoring morale." Mrs. T smoothed her shawl.

Tammy grinned, unrepentant. "Purely for research purposes. Potential romance writer, maybe one day."

Romance writer? I'm still waiting on your first cozy mystery you promised I could launch at the store.

"We caught a solid 'thunk.'" Tammy held up fingers counting off. "An 'ow,' some mutual apologies, and potentially forehead-to-doorframe contact. Then a nervous laugh duet that could melt snow."

Olivia buried her face in her palms. "You heard all that?"

"Every sound," Tammy said. "Textbook slow burn and pure gold. We were missing visuals, though. Before the next encounter, you should install a peephole in this bookshelf or in a painting, like in old movies where the eyes follow people. Strictly investigative."

Lockie chirped, tail curling as if co-signing the plan.

Mrs. T gave a sage nod. "Young love and criminal conspiracies both require observation. For entirely different reasons."

Olivia flung her arms skyward, laughter bubbling out despite herself. "I can't decide which of you is worse."

Tammy scribbled an imaginary note in the air. "Title suggestion: The Glazier, the Bookstore, and the Cat Who Knew Too Much."

"A bit long, dear, but accurate."

Olivia sank onto a stool, heat still radiating from her cheeks. "You've had your fun. Let's get back to the murder."

CHAPTER 19

Olivia flipped open her notebook. "All right, team, minus Xander and Wally, let's get back to our regularly scheduled murder."

Mrs. T stirred her tea. "You do make it sound fun, dear."

Olivia crossed to the evidence board. At the center sat a photograph of the necklace, ringed with letters signed under code names and sticky notes in various hands.

"Margaret Taylor cleans the post office. Her husband isn't always with her. She could easily explain the extra time taken around this time of year on having to dust the Christmas Village when what she's really doing is steaming open the Jeremiah and Gwendolyn letters."

Mrs. T set down her spoon. "If she's been doing it for years, she would only have to steam open the one new letter, having already read the rest."

"Mr. Taylor did say she had theories," Tammy said. "Maybe they're based on what she's already read."

The bell above the bookstore door chimed. Footsteps hurried through the stacks, and Wally appeared in the doorway, cheeks flushed from the cold. He unwound his scarf.

"Sorry I'm late. Bell ringing practice for the Tree Lighting. Della Mae wanted perfect timing before we could leave." He paused. "What did I miss?"

"Margaret Taylor is a suspect," Olivia said.

Wally blinked. "The postmaster's wife?"

Tammy gestured him closer to the board where Olivia had added her name under the heading *Suspects*. "She has access to the letters, and today she practically interrogated me in the square."

"Don't forget the peppermint." Mrs. T lifted her cup. "Margaret offered Tammy peppermint bark this afternoon. From a tin she carries in her handbag."

Wally crossed his arms. "That's... circumstantial at best."

"It's a pattern," Tammy said. "Opportunity, behavior, and a physical trace that matches. Not proof, but enough to keep an eye on her."

"She could know something we don't," said Olivia.

Wally rubbed his jaw. "Can we consider her a possible ally?"

No one answered. Lockie stretched on the table, claws flexing against the wood.

The words "Chicago, PI" stood out on the board. "If Henry hired Morton, he could be either scared he's next or feeling guilty about something else, like killing him."

Wally shifted his weight. "Or if Morton was killed because of what he found, and Henry set him on the trail, that's a heavy burden to carry."

"The necklace matters to Henry," Tammy said.

"And the letters that Margaret may have read all mention an object and so forth," Olivia said. "Could it be the ruby necklace? Could Henry be Jeremiah and the woman in the photo Gwendolyn?"

"That's a theory and a half, dear." Mrs. T sipped her tea.

"What if Margaret is Gwendolyn and she opened them because she knew they were for her?" Tammy pressed her palms against the table. "But she can't have the necklace, can she?"

"If they were working together and hired Morton, who was killed, they could be worried about being next," said Olivia.

Wally pushed off from the wall. "Or they both suspect the other did it."

"Margaret can't be Gwendolyn if the letters are for her. That would make her Jeremiah," Olivia pointed out.

Tammy rubbed her temples. "I think we're all losing it."

No one disagreed.

Mrs. T stood, gathering her things. "Dinner at the Swinging Spoon, then bed. We can resume tomorrow."

Wally grabbed his scarf from the chair. "Some fuel and distance will do us good. It's been a long day."

Olivia huffed a short breath. "We found a dead body this morning."

Mrs. T headed through the door. "Just another day in Willowcroft."

CHAPTER 20

After a twenty-minute drive, Olivia pushed through the door of Sugarplum Confectionery. The store smelled like Christmas had been distilled into the air, all warm sugar, melted cocoa, and buttercream swirling beneath the *Jingle Bells* carol. Shelves gleamed with ribboned jars of fudge, and the pink-and-white striped walls practically shimmered under the glow of the fairy lights.

"Olivia!" Nora, the owner, called, her brown curls tied up in a candy-cane scarf. "You're just in time. I was about to call you."

Olivia lifted a parcel. "No need. One *Twelve Teas of Christmas* for your mother, straight from Bookworm Haven's specialty order desk." She slid it across the counter. "I also dropped off a new western at the bakery."

"You're a lifesaver." Nora took the book, cradling it to her chest. "I was worried it wouldn't arrive in time."

The chocolatey air filled Olivia's lungs. "Speaking of stock, have you sold much of those peppermint-centered pieces? The ones in gold foil with the red snowflake pattern?"

"Oh, the Winterberry Delights?" Nora's whole face lit up. "One of our best sellers. I've gone through two full crates this week. You can't keep them on the shelf come December."

The lead crumbled. Olivia tucked that disappointment away with practiced grace.

"Probably half the county has eaten one. Want one for the road?"

Thanks for rubbing it in even more that I'm pursuing a dead end.

"I'd better not. But I will take a peppermint mocha."

"Coming right up." Nora already turned to the espresso machine. "For my favorite book courier."

Olivia drifted toward the front window. A display of sugar-dust-coated truffles arranged like tiny snowballs filled the sill.

The door banged open.

A man in a dark parka stomped in, chewing loudly. "Need a dozen Winterberry Delights. Pack them quick. I'm busy."

Nora startled but obeyed, scooping the requested sweets into a box.

"Olivia, your mocha for the drive back to Willowcroft will be ready in a minute," Nora called over her shoulder.

The man scowled at Olivia.

Before Nora tied the ribbon, he snatched the box, tossed a crumpled bill onto the counter, and barreled out the door—straight into Sheriff Stanton.

The impact jolted both men. The candies wobbled, then clattered to the ground, scattering gold-wrapped pieces across the entryway. Lamby barked once in surprise, then sneezed a single sharp puff, followed by two quick, snuffling sneezes as he sniffed the fallen treats. Stanton tugged the leash.

"Easy, boy." He squinted at the departing man as he hurried down the street. "Well, that was charming."

"He's new in town," Nora said. "And unfortunately, becoming a regular."

"A customer's a customer." Olivia stepped forward to pat Lamby. "I see you two make dramatic entrances. And bless you, Lamby."

Stanton glared at his dog. "The sneezes are a new development."

Olivia giggled. "A seasonal allergy?"

Stanton stooped to collect a sweet and a gum wrapper. "We'll see what the vet says." His gaze locked on her. "What brings you all the way to Oaktown?"

Her mouth opened, but Nora beat her to it.

"She hand-delivered my mother's Christmas present." Nora slid the mocha across the counter. "Which is why this is on the house."

Olivia accepted it. "Perks of the book trade."

Stanton raised a brow. "Convenient timing. I hope this little delivery doesn't have anything to do with your other… interests."

She took a sip, letting the mint and chocolate swirl together before replying. "If by 'interests' you mean Christmas shopping, absolutely."

He didn't look convinced. Lamby sneezed again, almost on cue, and then sat politely, tail thumping once against Olivia's boot as if greeting an old friend.

Olivia crouched to scratch his chin. "How's the case going? Did it bring you here to Sugarplum Confectionery?"

"Can't comment on an ongoing investigation."

"Of course not," Olivia said, smiling into her cup. "But I'll keep my ears open anyway."

"Why am I not surprised?"

Lamby's nose hovered near Olivia's mocha, then sneezed again.

Stanton gestured toward the door. "Safe travels back to Willowcroft. Roads are icing up."

The dismissal couldn't have been clearer if he had escorted her out by the elbow.

Olivia stepped outside. The sheriff waited until she'd cleared the porch before turning back to Nora, his expression shifting into something more serious.

Guess I'm not wanted. So much for friendly conversation.

She walked to her car. The trip had yielded nothing useful for Morton's murder. The candy wrapper could've belonged to anyone in Michigan with a sweet tooth, which the sheriff was about to find out.

She sipped the mocha anyway. At least it was warm and scrumptious.

CHAPTER 21

Flurries clung to Tammy's scarf like sequins as she stepped into the square. The town had transformed. The Christmas Market glittered with every stall trimmed with ribbons and fir. Garlands looped from lampposts, bells jingled with every passing gust, and somewhere a brass band was attempting *Ding Dong Merrily on High* slightly off-key.

Children dragged parents toward the giant spruce. Vendors called cheerful greetings. Normal life continued in true Willowcroft style, with candy canes as signposts and the faint hum of gossip in the air.

It was snow-globe perfection. Something must have gone right after the disaster the square had been when she'd spoken to Henry Beaumont.

She paused beside a hot chocolate stand. The scent of hazelnut cream curled around her. She could almost forget they were investigating a murder instead of just undeliverable letters.

Tammy pulled out her notebook, its pages smudged from yesterday's chaos. Someone here now could be a killer. How do peppermint, rubies, and Christmas cards connect?

A flash of color caught her attention. Mere yards away, the vibrant hues were unmistakable.

She inched closer. A tall, broad-shouldered man unpacked boxes. Beside him, a woman with gray roots directed the placement of skeins.

"The 'Winter Solstice' line goes front and center, David," the woman instructed.

Tammy's fingers twitched, itching to touch the yarn. "That's a stunning display."

The man, David, apparently, pivoted. The wary set of his shoulders held, but he smoothed his expression into something courteous. "Thank you," he replied.

"First time at the Willowcroft Christmas Market?"

The woman smiled. "Yes, actually. I'm Claire, and this is my husband, David. We're based in Grand Rapids, but we thought we'd branch out."

Tammy opened her mouth to ask another question when David winced and nearly dropped a box.

"Careful, honey! Those cuts are fresh."

David grimaced, flexing his bandaged hands. "Craft knife accident."

Injured hands, yarn matching the crime scene...

Tammy forced herself to maintain a casual demeanor. She drifted to a nearby stand, pretending to be interested in hand-carved ornaments while keeping the stall in view.

A middle-aged woman approached Claire. "These colors are gorgeous!"

Claire's hands fluttered over the display. "It's my signature blend—alpaca and silk."

"Can I find this anywhere else?" the customer asked.

"Exclusive to online and now the Willowcroft Christmas Market."

David positioned himself at the corner of the booth, his stance reminiscent of the off-duty cops Tammy interviewed for her novels: weight balanced, exits mapped, crowd assessed.

Ex-law enforcement? Former military? Thug for hire?

She approached the stall again and ran her fingers over a skein. "I'm working on a mystery novel set in a small town. Maybe I'll include a yarn artisan character."

David's muscles coiled at the word "mystery." Claire's hands darted to straighten already perfect displays. "I'd love to tell you about the craft!"

She launched into an explanation of yarn-making techniques. Tammy kept David in her peripheral vision. His protective stance and hyper-awareness seemed at odds with the cozy market atmosphere.

What's his story?

Tammy feigned interest. "How long have you been dyeing yarn?"

"Five years now. It started as a hobby and just... blossomed."

David shifted his weight, his focus alternating between Tammy and the market entrance. Her fingers itched to jot down notes, but she resisted.

"First time in Willowcroft, you said?"

David squared his shoulders and grunted in acknowledgment. As he lifted a delicate display stand from its packaging, a wince flashed across his face.

"Those cuts giving you trouble?"

David cleared his throat.

Tammy's internal alarm bells clanged.

"Paper cuts are my occupational hazard. Every trade has one, I guess."

David concentrated on unpacking, ignoring Tammy.

"I'm sorry your first time in Willowcroft was after that unfortunate incident yesterday."

His shoulders tensed, his movements stilted.

"It's shocking." Claire's fingers knotted in the yarn.

"Were you in town last night?"

"Grand Rapids." David's reply was clipped. "Market prep."

Claire's hands froze mid-fold. A heartbeat passed. "Yes... preparing."

The hesitation was brief but unmistakable.

"A long night, I imagine."

David wandered out the back, disappearing from view.

A booming voice interrupted from the next stand over. "That Morton fella was asking about some ruby necklace."

Another vendor popped her head around a rack of scarves. "The body was that guy? The one asking about the family at the inn? The expensive coat?"

"That's how I heard it," the first replied. "Funny thing though. There were two of them, one right after the other. One was polite, said 'thank you, ma'am,' and all that. The other..." She wrinkled her nose. "Rude as sin. Chomping gum like a cow and smelled of tobacco and peppermint. He only asked about the family."

"Couldn't tell which one was which when the news broke. Nice one's dead, rude one's probably still out there chewing."

A third vendor joined in, wiping her hands on a dish towel. "You sure it wasn't the same man twice?"

"What do you take me for?" the scarf-seller said. "I saw two different fellas. One with manners, one with breath that'd melt tinsel."

From the cider van came another voice, older and certain. "You're all wrong. There were three. I'm sure of it. The polite one walked off with someone else, not the smelly one in the dark parka. I saw him."

The scarf-seller laughed. "Three? You need your eyes checked."

But the vendor shook her head, stubborn. "I'm telling you, there were three. The smelly one was last. He dropped a gum wrapper. I had to pick it up myself. Some people have no respect."

Tammy snagged on the word peppermint.

A new vendor ducked around her display. "Does Henry know about this?"

Tammy feigned innocence. "What does it have to do with Henry?"

David reappeared.

"That man was asking about the Beaumont necklace that disappeared thirty years ago."

"Do you think the person who took it is still in town?"

"Nah, it was that family staying at the inn who did a flit in the middle of the night. Why else would you leave during a blizzard?"

David's spine snapped straight. His fingers dug into Claire's shoulder, a signal that could land as comfort or warning.

He knows something about that family.

"Truck," David said. "Need to move it." He strode away, his wallet half slipping from his back pocket as he shoved his hands into his coat. Claire's fingers twisted yarn into knots.

Wind gusted through the stalls, sending papers dancing. Tammy brushed hair from her face and edged back from the yarn table, eyes still on Claire and the gap where David had been.

Time to update the murder board.

CHAPTER 22

Tammy shouldered through the front door. The bell jangled. She barged through the hidden door. Lockie darted in at her heels, tail high, a streak of determination in fur form. "We are going to need a bigger board!"

"What's happening?" Mrs. T startled awake from a nap.

"Suspects galore." Tammy removed the copied letters from the whiteboard side.

Lockie leapt onto a nearby chair.

Olivia's head popped up from behind a carton of Christmas stock. "Slow down."

"I can't." Tammy uncapped a marker. "I have to get it down before it tangles." She huffed and puffed. "I met the owners of the yarn stall and received excellent intel from market vendor chat. They mentioned three different men."

She sucked a breath. Wally nudged the secret door shut. "Tell us what you heard first, then what you think."

Tammy drew four clean columns. At the top, she wrote, in blocky capitals:

ONE | TWO / MORTON | THREE | DAVID

Olivia hugged herself, grinning. "We have real suspects!"

Tammy raised the pen to the first column. "All of this is what they said." She wrote, reading aloud as she went.

"One. Rude. Short. Smelly: peppermint, tobacco. Gum chewing. Asked about family only. Dark parka."

Lockie hopped up and began batting at a marker lid, skidding it across the table. The clatter made everyone glance over; Lockie froze, wide-eyed, then resumed his pawing with exaggerated innocence.

"Next is two, which is Morton. He's dead, but we need to map the others in relation to him."

She resumed writing, speaking as she went.

"Polite. Tall. Asking about the necklace and family." She underlined the "and" before moving on. "Expensive coat."

She turned to face the team. "I'm skipping to David."

"Who's that?" asked Mrs. T.

"That's the husband of the Winter Solstice yarn artisan, Claire."

"The yarn from the crime scene?" asked Olivia.

"Yes. Claire said it was their first time in Willowcroft. But he flinched when the inn family was mentioned, like he knew them, but how? He didn't react to the necklace."

She continued writing on the murder board.

"Query ex-law enforcement based on the way he stood and scanned the crowd. He had fresh cuts on his hands, supposedly from a craft knife accident."

"They are very sharp," said Mrs. T.

"Or he got them during the struggle with Morton before killing him," said Wally.

"Now to corroboration of the sightings as not all vendors agreed." Tammy pointed at the first and second columns. "One and two are clear individuals, with everyone agreeing on seeing them and their details."

"Number Three was only seen by the cider vendor, who saw him with Morton on the day of the murder. That's all I have for him."

Between Three and David, she added a big question mark and two thin arrows pointing both ways.

"My working theory is that they might be the same person. This stays tentative until we prove it."

Lockie let out a soft chirp that sounded suspiciously like agreement.

"What makes you think they are the same person?" Wally asked.

"The cider vendor is further away from David and Claire. She never said anything about him asking questions, just that he was with Morton."

She drew a rough plan of the market and circled the vendors close to the yarn stall.

"What if these stallholders didn't consider David someone to mention because they knew him from a neighboring booth?"

She pointed to the van at the end of the row.

"Whereas the cider vendor may see David as part of the crowd. Given the distance and the fact David comes and goes, which I saw myself while talking with Claire. It's possible."

Wally sat forward. "If we can merge Three and David, that would give us one less suspect and place David with the victim, who was found with his wife's yarn fiber."

"And finally, Henry needs to be included. We know he hired Morton to find the necklace and assume he suspects the family of having stolen it, along with everyone else in town."

Tammy stepped back from the board to examine her work. "I saw him with Morton at the cemetery. He's gone from distracted to strange since Morton died, and he refused to tell me where he was that night."

"What about their movements over the last few days?" asked Wally.

"That's it from the market chatter." Tammy started writing under ONE again. "But short, dark parka matches my cemetery guy, who seemed interested in Morton more than in Henry and drove off in the red Toyota.

That places him in town three days before the murder, with sightings on the day of the murder."

Lockie sneezed dramatically, sending a scattering of notes to the floor.

"He potentially fits the rude guy at Oaktown this morning," piped up Olivia. "And *he* bought Winterberry Delights—the wrapper found at the crime scene."

Tammy added that underneath One and moved on to Two.

"I saw Morton at the cemetery; he helped with the Nutcracker, and Marjorie saw him at the Beaumont estate."

"That places him in town four days before he died, or five days ago," said Olivia.

Mrs. T picked up her vibrating phone. "I asked Georgina if any of the guests at the hotel had registered a red Toyota. She said no."

"So, maybe One is staying at the Oaktown Inn, which makes sense if he was seen at Sugarplum," surmised Tammy.

"On the night of the murder, One, Two, Three, David, and Henry were all in town," said Wally.

"That means they all had the opportunity without any concrete alibis as yet," said Olivia. "Not that Morton needs an alibi for his own death."

Everyone was in deep thought except Mrs. T, who said, "Motive is the tricky one."

Olivia picked up the letter printouts from the table. "What about these? What about 1995?"

Wally walked over to the board. "We know Henry was in town back then. Morton would have been in his late twenties."

"That sounds about the right age for David too," said Tammy.

"Oaktown guy looked too young for anything more than play dates in '95," offered Olivia.

"What about Margaret's interest in the letters?" asked Mrs. T.

"I can't see any potential connection between her and anyone but Henry, and that's only because they both live in town," said Wally.

"First, we need to confirm if David is Three," said Tammy. "That would eliminate one suspect."

Olivia looked at each in turn. "Do we know the cider vendor?"

Mrs. T sighed. "Alas, no. She's from Stonefield."

Tammy scanned the room. "Where's Xander? We need his long lens camera."

"Finals," Mrs. T said.

"Right."

"Nick Bradley," Olivia said, already reaching for her phone. "We know he has photography skills."

"He's got finals too, dear," Mrs. T added.

"Dang," Tammy said. "We need a clear photo of David to take to the cider vendor and ask if he's Three."

Olivia jumped up, all excited. "Easy! We pretend to take a selfie in front of the stall opposite, but don't put the phone in selfie mode, meaning it will show David without him knowing."

Tammy was halfway out the door. "Let's do it."

She stopped. "David will recognize me."

"Not with a balaclava and your coat hood up." Olivia fished out a black woolen item from a drawer in the kitchenette.

Tammy put it over her head. "Why didn't you wear this the night of the post office?"

Olivia shrugged.

Tammy yanked her coat from the wall hook, pulling the hood as low as she could, and practically jogged out into the cold, Olivia at her heels.

Lockie trotted beside them, tail high, fur dusted with a few stray flakes as the air bit sharp with snow and wood smoke. The Christmas market had gotten busier, *Santa Claus Is Coming to Town* rang out from near the fountain, strings of colored bulbs blinking in the dusk. Every direction was a scene from a storybook, but Tammy's eyes were on the Winter Solstice yarn hut and the man unpacking skeins.

Olivia had her phone poised. "Ready?"

"Let's pretend we want samples and then take fake selfies with the fudge pyramids."

Olivia mimed shivering, dramatic and loud, and David turned to look. They posed. Snap. Snap. Snap. If he recognized Tammy, he didn't show it.

They played tourist for a few more selfies, then ran toward the cider van. They joined the line and checked their photos to find the best one, zooming in on David's face.

The vendor was stirring a hidden vessel inside the van, sending up ribbons of steam that smelled of cranberry and clove. Her hair was pulled into a loose braid, and she wore a faux fur vest, sleeves dusted with what could be nutmeg.

Tammy removed the balaclava. The woman glanced at Tammy, then at Olivia, then at Tammy again, lips twitching in recognition.

"Four Christmas Specials, please," Olivia said, as if this were a perfectly normal number for two people. The vendor nodded, sloshing spicy liquid into paper cups.

Lockie sniffed at the sweet-spiced steam, then hopped onto a nearby crate, curling his tail neatly around his paws like a furry stakeout partner.

Tammy angled her phone so the screen could be seen by the vendor but not by anyone behind her. "I was wondering if this is the third guy you saw with the smelly and polite ones?"

The photo showed David's face turned enough for a clear shot, brow tense, jaw tight.

The vendor snorted, coughed once, and then said, "If that's not him, I'll eat my apron. He was with the polite one." She pointed with her paddle, cider dripping to the cup below. "None of the others believed me."

Olivia paid for the drinks. "We believe you."

The next in line glared at them, so they skedaddled back to the store.

It seemed everyone in the market followed them into the bookstore, wanting to browse and purchase books. The bell jingled over and over, barely stopping between entries.

Wally and Mrs. T came out to see what the bell was doing and realized it was all hands on deck.

"Let's make this place run smoother than Santa's workshop," said Wally.

Their cider would have to wait.

In minutes, they became a well-oiled festive machine. Wally manned the scanner with surprising efficiency, Olivia handled payments, and Mrs. T and Tammy alternated between bagging and wrapping, chatting with customers about gift ideas.

Lockie supervised from under the counter, occasionally hopping up to place one approving paw on a freshly wrapped package or watching Olivia's transactions with hawk-like seriousness.

When the line finally dwindled, Olivia rang up the last sale and exhaled, pushing a stray lock of hair behind her ear. "Thanks for the help, everyone. It's going to be a bumper season."

They shared a weary but satisfied glance. The kind that said they'd earned their next clue.

Lockie yawned and stretched, curling himself atop the receipt pile like a giant paperweight.

Amid the busyness, the gleaming new window framed a perfect view of the market. They'd been hiding out back, but from here they could stake out the comings and goings from the warmth of the store.

Despite the darkness growing deeper, Tammy could see the potential.

"Tomorrow I propose we start Operation Christmas Window."

"I'm in!" said Olivia.

Tammy loved her ever-enthusiastic and curious friend. "I haven't even told you what it is."

"Doesn't matter. I'm there!"

"Tomorrow we stay in the store with prime viewing of the market. It will look as though we are stocking, cleaning, and helping customers, all while we watch out the window."

Mrs. T raised an eyebrow. "Is that inspired by your adventure with my telescope? Shall I bring it?"

"That might be a bit conspicuous, although we could set it up in the window, pretending it's getting ready to catch Santa arriving."

"Santa Cam. I love it!" Olivia beamed.

"Minus the camera," Mrs. T added.

"We have a good view of the fountain and the first double row of stalls." Tammy moved to the far right. "From the corner, I can just see the cider van. Now that Three is confirmed as David, we are down to three suspects, two of whom are guaranteed to be around the market and the other who has previously been seen in the vicinity."

Olivia bounced on her toes. "This is awesome!"

Chapter 23

The next morning, Tammy marched into Bookworm Haven, half-blinded by her own breath cloud and the milky sunrise reflecting off the snow piled on the window ledges.

Olivia was stationed at the front counter, humming *Santa Baby* (badly, off-key, utterly unselfconscious), wrestling a two-foot cardboard sign through a tangle of tinsel. Across the top, in bold candy-cane stripes, it blazed: "SANTA CAM—LIVE SLEIGH MONITORING TODAY!" Underneath was a child's drawing of a stick-figure Santa being stalked by a telescope.

Olivia spotted her. "It's beautiful, right?"

Tammy blinked. "It's...big."

"All the best lies start out loud." Olivia threaded the string through a suction hook and slapped it on the main window.

Mrs. T swept in with Wally behind her, lugging a large case.

He unpacked the telescope. Metal legs locked, the tube settled, and the lens cap came away. Tammy stepped nearer, her heart ticking fast. The others edged in until their shoulders touched.

"This thing has more power than half the traffic cams in the county." Wally gave it a gentle tap.

Olivia clapped, as if it might start reading bedtime stories.

Tammy took the eyepiece first. It was strange how quickly the telescope shrank the distance between herself and the suspects. Overnight, the market had become a chessboard. Vendors in puffy jackets sipped coffee and blinked in the new sun. Shoppers drifted from booth to booth, their bags ballooning with presents and decorations.

She panned the scope slowly, passing over the fudge stand and the edge of the cider van, but the angle blocked any sight of the yarn stall.

Wally sifted closer. "Look for our Mr. One."

Tammy bit her bottom lip and scanned the crowd. Smelly Peppermint Guy, as she'd started thinking of him, would hopefully show.

A small herd of kids, five or six, had gathered at the window, faces pressed to the glass. A little kid, bundled in a NASA-logo parka, pointed at the telescope with visible awe. Olivia gave him a thumbs up and opened the door enough to say, "Want to try it? You can watch for Santa's test flights."

The kid gave her a look, part suspicion, part hope. He stepped in, boots squeaking, with parents trailing behind him.

Tammy watched Olivia walk him through the scope's controls, showing him how to pan left and right and how to focus.

He immediately zeroed in on the giant inflatable Santa perched on the roof of Mrs. Hubbard's Cupboard. "He's not moving," he observed, matter-of-factly.

"He's resting up for the big night," Olivia deadpanned.

The parents laughed. "Can I see too?" asked the mom, already leaning in.

"Knock yourself out." Tammy swept her hand in a game show gesture.

While the family took turns at the telescope, she snuck a couple peeks herself.

No sign of smelly man.

Lockie, who'd commandeered the footstool beneath the front window, sprawled out, unbothered by the human drama.

"Santa Cam is bringing in great foot traffic," said Mrs. T. "Brilliant marketing."

Olivia raised her arms. "All part of the plan. It may become a tradition."

At least the store was reaping rewards from Santa Cam, unlike the investigation. There were a few David sightings here and there, coming and going as usual. Henry did the rounds over and over, supervising the overall running of the market, but nothing suspicious was observed from either of them.

The Christmas tree in the far corner towered over the stalls. Archie Beaumont and the other dressers were getting closer to the top. It was nearly ready for the lighting.

Wally had slipped out to bell practice for the big night.

Xander had texted saying finals were going well and there were no new pings on the necklace or the woman wearing it.

It seemed they'd hit a dead end.

Without knowing what Mr. One looked like, he could have walked past the store a dozen times, and they wouldn't have known. They needed to invent a "smell cam" to catch him.

Tammy took another look while no one was waiting in line to track Santa. Nothing, but something on the ground caught her eye. A bit of color against the white.

Being so close, the image was blurred, but there was something there. Snow didn't come in technicolor.

"I'm heading outside for a minute."

Olivia gave her a quick wave as she served a customer.

At the entrance to the middle row lay a photograph.

She looked around. Anyone could have dropped it at any time.

Tammy scooped it up.

The picture showed a family of three—mom, dad, and a teenage girl with a rebellious smirk. They stood in what was unmistakably the reception area of the Willowcroft Inn, its grand staircase curving behind them. The timestamp said 1995. Tammy flipped the photo over, her breath catching as she read the single word scrawled on the back: "Winters."

"No way," she whispered, her attention drawn back to the image. That's when she spotted him. A fourth person in the background, his face partially obscured but still recognizable. Here, in town, decades ago.

Chapter 24

Tammy crammed the photo into her mitten and rushed back to the bookstore. She was halfway through the door before she realized she had carried snow in on her boots, leaving a trail like some caroling raccoon. She ignored it.

Olivia, mid-customer, threw a brow waggle. "Find Santa?"

"Better." Tammy made a beeline for the back. She paused to snag Mrs. T from the history shelf and gestured Wally over with a jerk of her chin.

They slipped through the disguised bookshelf into their secret workspace. Lockie slunk in behind and nosed at the hem of Tammy's jeans. She set the photo face down on the table. Faded ink spelled out "Winters" across the back.

The group huddled closer, a collective gasp.

"Turn it over," Wally said.

Tammy flipped it. Light glinted off the surface, illuminating the family frozen in the frame.

Olivia tapped each figure. "John, Mary, and Sarah."

"Timestamped thirty years ago," Wally said.

Tammy jabbed her finger at the fourth person.

Olivia turned to Mrs. T. "Your magnifying glass?"

Mrs. T pulled it from her knitting bag and handed it over.

Olivia studied the photo through the lens.

Xander pushed through the door.

"Is that David?" Olivia asked.

"In Willowcroft. 1995. With the inn family." Tammy's fingers traced the edges. "No wonder he flinched when the vendors mentioned them."

Lockie gave a satisfied purr, as if agreeing, and twined around Tammy's legs while the others stared at the photo.

A scream split the air.

Lockie bolted for the hidden door, fur spiking.

"What in heaven's name—?" Mrs. T startled.

Wally sprang up.

They burst into the bookstore. Every customer stood stock-still, pages mid-turn, faces toward the square as another scream pierced the quiet.

"Move," Tammy said.

What did we miss in those few minutes?

They plunged into the cold. A mass of people gathered at the Christmas market's far end.

Vendors stretched to see. Empty booths marked where others had abandoned their posts. The growing knot of bodies ahead spoke volumes. *Something's wrong. Very wrong.*

They pushed through the crowd. Lockie darted between legs. Claire stood rooted before her stall, palms pressed to her face, skin chalk-white. Yarn spools littered the ground.

A leg stuck out from under the back curtain leading to the service passage.

Tammy's mouth went desert-dry. She inched forward and lifted the fabric.

Henry Beaumont sprawled across the cobblestones, eyes vacant, strands of Winter Solstice yarn tangled around one hand.

Mrs. T sucked in a breath. Olivia's fingers dug into Tammy's sleeve.

"He wasn't—" Claire shook. "I stepped away. For change."

Sheriff Stanton and Deputy Brown muscled through the crowd. Lamby trotted beside them, tail high. A stranger shadowed them.

"Back up, folks," the sheriff said.

Lamby halted at the forming line, nose working. A whine escaped him as he sat by the sheriff, ears forward, fixed on the scene.

From the crowd's edge, Lockie crouched low, tail flicking once. His focus locked on Lamby, measuring the newcomer. Lamby turned his head, ears pricking, and for a heartbeat, they stared each other down, cat wary and dog calm, before Lamby huffed and sat by Stanton. Lockie stayed at Tammy's boots, still and watchful, as if conceding a temporary truce.

Deputy Brown strung yellow tape between stalls. Claire stumbled back, palm pressed to her sternum.

Tammy cataloged details: the body's position, scattered yarn, dark stains on stone that forced her to look away.

Wally guided her to the crowd's edge.

Claire stood unsteady, tears tracking down her face as Stanton scribbled in his notepad.

Lamby sniffed the curtain's edge where yarn pooled. At Stanton's signal, he backed away with three sharp sneezes. His ears remained pricked.

"Where's the husband?" Wally asked.

Tammy scanned faces. "Not here."

"He's missing?" Olivia said.

David materialized on their left, gripping two cups in bandaged hands. He slowed at the yellow tape, the crowd, the body. Claire's posture softened at his approach.

His jaw tensed as he passed her a cup, his free hand hovering near her back. *Protective? Or guilty?*

Mrs. T tugged Tammy's sleeve. "Time to go, dears. We have much to discuss."

The sheriff's words carried over the whispers. Lockie's ears twitched at the sound before he gave a chirp that signaled time to go. Tammy turned toward Bookworm Haven, Lockie padding beside her.

Tammy entered last. Olivia locked the front door and changed the sign to CLOSED behind her. *We don't need customers right now.*

Mrs. T took charge with quiet efficiency. "Tea, I think. Strong and sweet. We all need it."

Tammy dropped into the nearest chair. "Let's watch from here, though, so we don't miss anything else."

Lockie sat in the window, alert.

Wally paced, his scarf still hanging loose. "David was missing when they found Henry."

"Then he turned up carrying coffee." Olivia pressed her back against the counter.

"That bothers me," Wally said.

"Did anyone see that third guy with the Sheriff and Deputy Brown?" Tammy asked.

"I did," Wally said. "He had Fed written all over him."

What? "Thomas joked about a federal agent being in town. At least I thought he was joking."

"Incoming." Olivia dashed to unlock the door as the sheriff barreled through it with Lamby by his side.

She patted the dog. "Hello there, young man. Have you been to the vet yet about your sneezing?"

Stanton's jaw tightened. "Allergies, like you suspected." He cleared his throat. "I hear you've been playing with telescopes again." He jerked his chin toward the one in the window. "Please tell me you witnessed the murder."

Everyone shifted in their seats before Wally said, "Sorry, Stanton, we heard the scream from the back room."

The sheriff's shoulders sagged. "Unfortunate timing." He blew a long exhale out through his nose. "Anything you need to tell me?" His gaze pinged between them—Wally, Mrs. T, Olivia, Xander, and Tammy—like a searchlight.

Wally crossed his arms. "Nothing you don't already know. We saw both bodies the same as you."

"Are you certain?" Stanton's fists found his hips.

Mrs. T returned with a tea tray. "If we had something concrete, you'd be the first to know, Sheriff. None of us want a third tragedy before Christmas Eve. Can I offer you some tea?"

Stanton's right brow lifted in a way Tammy didn't think she could replicate.

Mrs. T poured and passed around hot mugs.

Olivia piped up. "Did you find anything connecting to Morton's murder?"

Stanton pursed his mouth, then angled his head, almost as if considering how much to give. "Too early to say if this was related to the first incident. Could be a tragic coincidence. Could be something else."

Tammy twisted a stray thread on her sleeve. *I hate not having all the pieces. Hate even more that maybe Stanton knows more than he's letting on.*

"We'll keep our noses clean," Wally said. "If it helps, we're convinced this is about that necklace."

"Of course it's related to the case you asked me about even before the first murder." He spun on his heels and returned to the new crime scene.

Olivia wrapped her hands around her tea, blowing on the steam. "Let's look at what we actually know. Morton was killed first. He was investigating the ruby. Now Henry Beaumont, who was obsessed with that necklace and hired Morton, is dead, too."

"Claire's yarn at both scenes," Tammy added. "And the photograph tells us David was in Willowcroft in 1995 when the necklace disappeared."

"Did you see who dropped the photo?" Mrs. T asked.

Tammy's shoulders deflated. "No. It could have been anyone in the market."

"Could Morton have found it and given it to Henry?" Olivia asked.

"Henry walked past multiple times, but so did David," Tammy said. "Neither of them stands still well."

"It doesn't exactly look as if David wants to be in the photo," Wally said. "So why keep it and why have it with him today?"

Mrs. T lowered her teacup. "So we're thinking Henry dropped the photo?"

Olivia framed the air with both hands, director style.

"In a town blanketed in white," she said in her deep movie trailer baritone, "two men meet under the pines. One, a client with a restless conscience. The other, a private investigator with proof." She fanned two fingers as if holding photos. "Morton reveals not one, but two photographs. Gasp. The PI raises his price. Henry panics. Tempers rise. A shove. A stumble. The forest holds its breath."

She snatched one imaginary photo to her chest and mimed a sprint for the door. "Henry grabs a photo and runs." She clutched the second to her palm, fingers curling tight. "Morton clings to the other until his last heartbeat. Cut to snow falling. A still hand in the drift. Credits roll. Dun-dun-dun."

She sat back down and took a calm sip of her tea.

Tammy snickered.

Mrs. T muttered, "Overwrought, but serviceable."

Wally's eyebrow did the work of an entire jury before he said, "Payment dispute fits. Panic, a shove, unintended death. Still murder."

Tammy rubbed the edge of the print. "If Henry killed Morton, it would explain why he was so rattled."

"The photo gave him a reason to approach David," said Olivia. "And David came out on top."

Xander, who had been quiet, snapped to attention and dashed into the back room. The team followed.

He scanned the new image and zoomed in on it side by side with the first photo.

Everyone hovered closer.

Xander tapped the two images. "Look at the woman in Morton's picture. And now look at the teenager in the Winters family photo."

Tammy's pulse kicked. "It's her... Older, but definitely her."

A shadow of sadness crossed Mrs. T's expression before she spoke. "Which means the town was right. The Winters family did leave Willowcroft with the necklace."

"And Morton found the proof," said Olivia.

Xander's expression darkened. "What if Olivia's movie is a trilogy in which people who see the photo end up dead?"

Knock.

Knock.

Knock.

Chapter 25

No one moved. Lockie froze, ballooned to twice his size.

"Olivia?... It's Mike."

Air flooded back into Olivia's lungs. Mike. The security conversation he'd promised. Perfect timing. Also catastrophic.

"Don't let him see the board."

Four heads whipped to the murder board.

"Stall him," Wally said.

She crossed to the back door and gripped the bolt.

"Olivia?" Mike again, louder. "You there?"

Mrs. T yanked a heavy tablecloth from a drawer and flicked it open. She flung it over the spread of notes and maps. Papers and binders formed awkward hills beneath the fabric.

Lumpy. Too lumpy.

She pulled a second cloth. "The board."

Wally swept it over the tall wheeled frame like a magician covering a trick. The cloth stopped short of the floor. The outline of pins and string still showed if you knew where to look.

Mrs. T eased the kettle onto the front burner and twisted the knob.

Good idea. Steam will say we are civilized people having civilized tea. Not people mapping two murders.

Tammy slid errant printouts into a bakery box. Lockie hopped to the kitchenette counter and set a paw on the closed box like a tiny customs officer.

"Liv?" Mike called, softer now. "It's just me."

Just Mike. Her pulse kicked.

"Sorry," she called. "Back door sticks."

True until Xander fixed it. The bolt slid easily. She held it closed.

"Are we decent?"

"Decent adjacent." Xander smoothed the tablecloth. "Do it."

She cracked the door.

Mike filled the frame, cold air pooling at his boots, hair mussed from the wind. That boyish smile he forgot to hide when he looked at her.

"Hey," he said. "You okay?"

"We're fine." She opened wider to make it true. "You were coming to talk security, right?"

"Yeah." He glanced past her, taking in the back room. "Given today's developments, I thought sooner was better."

Her heart did a small, foolish turn as her stomach flipped. *Sooner was better. Not for the board.*

"Tea? We have tea."

"Sounds good."

She stepped aside. Everyone wore their most innocent faces. Mrs. T handed him a cup like a peace treaty. Wally dipped his chin, the portrait of a man who was definitely not hiding a conspiracy under fabric. Tammy found a smile that begged him not to look left. Xander studied the bakery box as if it contained the answers to his calculus final.

Mike's eyes moved to the table. He touched a small rise in the cloth with a knuckle. "You need an iron in here."

"Noted." Heat crawled up her neck.

His gaze slid to the tall cloth-draped shape. "What is that?"

"Holiday window display ideas in progress," she said. "No peeking."

He grinned, as if half convinced. "Got it. Trade secrets."

His focus landed on Lockie next. The cat stared back, regal and unblinking, paw still planted on the box.

"What's in there?"

"Croissants." *Please don't ask for one.*

He laughed. "I have never understood what all the fuss is about with croissants."

Her shoulders loosened. "More for Lockie. They're his favorite."

He took a sip of tea and set the cup down. "All right. Let's talk about beefing up the back door and the cameras out front."

CHAPTER 26

They slipped out of the back room, leaving Olivia and Mike to discuss security behind the bookshelf door. Tammy couldn't handle the Mike and Olivia romcom right now, but she did hope they'd skip the crisis section and jump straight to the happily ever after.

"We should open the store." Tammy started for the front. "Nothing says Christmas shopping like a dead body."

Xander peered through the large window. "Is the market still open?"

"They only ran crime scene tape around the two affected stalls."

Wally tucked his hands in his pockets. "It would be a tough call. I'm glad I'm the ex-sheriff." He moved toward the counter. "Let's make Olivia some money."

Mrs. T straightened a display of book-themed coasters. "Every sale helps with cameras and those glazier bills."

Tammy unlocked the door and flipped the sign to OPEN. Wally clicked on the lamp by the register.

Xander lingered near the front. "I'm going to head home and study. One more day of finals. Also, Ranger Dad is there with his guns and dart tranquilizers. You know—for the bears... and anyone who might want to kill me."

"Text when you're in," Tammy said.

He waved his phone. "Will do. If you need me, text."

"Go ace your finals," Mrs. T said.

He gave them a half-hearted salute and disappeared out the front door into the noise of the market and crime scene.

The rhythm came quickly. Mrs. T took the register, calm and unflappable. Wally patrolled the aisles, finding the high-stock titles without a ladder. Tammy set up at the wrapping station. Lockie hopped beside her and set a paw on the end of the paper roll, grave as a foreman.

The doorbell chimed steadily. Shoppers drifted in with flushed cheeks and questions. A grandmother wanted a large-print mystery for her sister. A teen asked for something moody with old libraries. A man needed the book with the blue cover and a dog, which was apparently unforgettable to everyone but him. Mrs. T rang them up. Wally fetched. Tammy folded, creased, and tied ribbons. The repetitiveness smoothed her thoughts. Paper whispered. Tape clicked. Lockie thumped each finished parcel with a gentle paw of approval.

The store phone rang.

"I've got it," Tammy said. She lifted the receiver. "Bookworm Haven, how can I—"

A voice slid through, wrong and even, flattened by a machine. "Stop digging into the letters. Or else."

Tammy scanned the window. No one was on their phone. *Really.* "Who is this?"

Silence.

A dead line.

She set the receiver down, careful not to fumble it. Heat from the lamp pressed against her cheek.

"All good?" Wally asked from the returns cart.

A customer waited with a tower of paperbacks and a hopeful smile. Tammy found the top book and pulled fresh paper toward her. "All good," she said, steady enough for the room.

Lockie's ears flattened. He stared at the phone and gave a small, unhappy chirrup.

The back door creaked open, soft but enough to pull every head up. Olivia stepped into the store, expression unreadable.

Wally paused mid-stack with a pile of returns. Mrs. T's hand froze above the register. Tammy stilled her scissors halfway through a ribbon curl. Even Lockie stopped batting at the tape dispenser.

No one spoke.

Olivia stood there, deadpan.

Tammy broke first. "So. How did it go?"

Olivia blinked once. "Let's just say I might need a new glazier."

"Good heavens. What happened?" asked Mrs. T.

Olivia glanced toward the counter where two browsers were flipping through cookbooks. Her mouth pressed thin.

Wally caught on. "Folks, we're closing for a quick stock check."

Mrs. T backed him up with her most grandmotherly tone. "Come back in fifteen minutes."

The customers gave confused smiles and drifted out with murmured goodbyes. The bell over the door jingled shut, leaving only the faint hum of the heater and Lockie's tail thumping against the counter.

Wally locked the front door and flipped the sign to CLOSED. "Talk."

Olivia sighed. "He was showing me a photo of someone dressed as Santa crouched at the bookstore door when the tablecloth fell off the murder board." She rubbed her temples. "One look at the frozen red marbling, and he balked and ran straight out the door."

Tammy winced. "Oh, Liv..."

Mrs. T crossed to her and rested a gentle hand on Olivia's arm. "You poor dear. Sit down before you faint."

Wally fetched a chair. "That man's got less stomach than a rookie deputy."

Olivia dropped into the seat and gave a short, humorless laugh. "Apparently."

Tammy gripped the edge of the display table. "Go back to the Santa bit."

Olivia looked up. "Mike said when he was out for an evening jog, he spotted someone in a Santa suit turning the doorknob. He thought it was some sort of prank until the guy bolted when he called out to him."

Wally's fingers drummed on his thigh. "Did he get a look at the face?"

"No. Just the suit and a flash of black boots."

Mrs. T tutted. "A burglar in a Santa costume. Merry Christmas."

Or a killer with a flair for holiday irony.

A sharp rap-rap-rap made them all jump. Two bundled-up shoppers peered through the frosted window, cupping their hands against the glass to see inside. One waved hopefully at the CLOSED sign.

Mrs. T straightened. "Duty calls."

Wally pushed to his feet. "You can't keep Christmas commerce waiting." He unlocked the door and swung it open.

"Come on in, folks. Just wrapping up some bookkeeping."

The customers bustled in, shaking off snow and chattering about last-minute gifts.

Tammy's face rearranged itself into something approximating a cheerful holiday wrapper. But between the Santa sighting and that phone call, the day had lurched into something far beyond cozy mystery.

They closed a little after seven, fixtures winking off one by one until a single counter lamp glowed. The market had thinned to strings of lights and the cleanup crew.

"Food." Wally grabbed his coat from the hook. "Before we start eating the gift wrap."

Olivia pulled on her scarf. "The Swinging Spoon? I'm famished."

They stepped next door. Warmth and the scent of char-grilled onions greeted them. They slid into their usual booth. The vinyl sighed.

The jukebox crooned Bing Crosby's *White Christmas* as Peggy glided across the checkered floor, balancing a tray laden with steaming plates.

After the menus, coffee, and the promise of meatloaf, Tammy recounted the call. By the time she reached the click at the end, Olivia's hand had gone still on the sugar packets.

"So we're back to the letters," Olivia said.

Tammy stared at the gloss of the tabletop. "Someone knows about them."

Wally set down his mug. "The only person who could know is Margaret."

Mrs. T cocked her head. "I have a hard time seeing Margaret sending threats."

Tammy's throat closed. *Thirty Christmases where a letter went nowhere.* "Gwendolyn might be writing about the necklace when she talks about the precious thing he gave her."

Wally traced a crack in the table. "What if Sarah Winters is Gwendolyn?"

Food arrived. Plates clattered. The diner buzzed around them.

Tammy picked up her fork. "All I know is someone cared enough about those letters to threaten us today."

"If David was in Willowcroft thirty years ago, maybe he's Jeremiah," said Olivia.

Wally cut into his meatloaf. "We don't have any leads on the letters. We should concentrate on David."

"I can talk to Claire again," Tammy said.

"And I'll follow her husband," Wally replied. "See what he does when wifey's not around."

Mrs. T reached for the salt. "That's our plan for tomorrow then."

Wally swallowed a bite. "And you're all staying at mine tonight."

"Yeah, yeah, we know." Olivia stabbed a green bean. "Because you're three doors down from the sheriff's department, safety in numbers, blah blah, been there, done that."

They ate. Silverware scraped plates. Peggy returned with the coffee pot and an offer of pie. "Sugar will refuel your detective brains."

Wally set down his fork. "You're an angel, Peggy. Sounds perfect. We'll have a whole one to go, please."

Tammy glanced at Lockie, snoozing beside her. "Let's get you packed. Who am I kidding? I don't need to pack for you. You already have a bed, food, and treats at Wally's house from our previous stays. Not to mention you have all of the above at the bookstore and Mrs. T's house. Xander's is the only place you haven't colonized. You know his mom's allergic, right?"

Lockie's ear twitched. His eyes stayed shut.

CHAPTER 27

By the time they reached Wally's house, no one had the energy for pie. They'd eaten it for breakfast instead.

The morning air bit sharply as they stepped out again, coffee steam still on their breath. Wally tugged his coat tight and scanned the market as if every snow-dusted hut might yield a clue. "David's on the move. You two talk to his wife. I'll follow him."

Tammy and Mrs. T split off, Lockie tucked into Tammy's arm like a purring travel mug. Claire had moved her unpacked stock to a stall abandoned by a spooked vendor. Skeins of yarn brightened the space, a fragile attempt at normalcy.

They visited the cider van first to grab three steaming cups of breakfast fruit punch. The sweet spice cut through the morning chill. Tammy gripped hers with both hands.

Claire rearranged her "Winter Solstice" display. Her fingers wavered each time she reached for a skein. She spotted them and straightened. "Can I help you?"

Tammy lifted her cup slightly. "Just checking in. Seeing how you're holding up."

Mrs. T joined her side. "It's been quite a shock for all of us, dear. Come have a hot punch with us for a few minutes."

Claire's mouth opened, then closed. She glanced from one woman to the other, then toward her half-unpacked crates. "I really should get up and running."

Tammy brushed a thumb across her cup, condensation cooling her glove. "You look like you could use a break."

Claire hesitated, then exhaled. The tension drained from her shoulders. "All right. Just for a bit."

They crossed to a bench near the fountain and handed her a punch. Claire's fingers curled around it, knuckles white. She'd slept through worry instead of rest, judging by the shadows beneath her eyes.

Tammy shifted forward. "Rough morning?"

Claire stared at the drink's surface. "It's David. He never talks about his past. I know he was in law enforcement, but he's so... closed off."

I knew it.

"When did you two meet?"

"Four years ago. After he retired." Steam blurred her expression. "He's been carrying something ever since. A shadow he can't shake."

Mrs. T reached across and clasped her hand. "Some men never stop carrying what they've seen on the job. Secrets weigh more than they realize."

Lockie hopped from Tammy's lap onto Claire's, curling up without hesitation. His quiet purr filled the pause.

The verdict is in. She's one of the good ones.

Claire smoothed his fur, and her words came out soft. "I love him so much. But lately he's been distant. Stressed. Something's closing in on him."

Tammy and Mrs. T exchanged a look of shared understanding. "Do you know where he was the night of the first murder?"

Claire dropped her head. "He told the sheriff he was home, but he wasn't. I don't know where he went. And now, with Mr. Beaumont..."

Her hand went to her throat. "He doesn't have an alibi for either of the murders. I can't stand thinking what it might mean."

Mrs. T rubbed small circles between her shoulder blades. "No one's accusing him, dear. We just need the truth so no one else gets hurt."

Sympathy tugged at Tammy despite the alarm bells clanging in her chest. "He's been jumpy, hasn't he? More than usual."

Claire drew a shaky breath. "Every sound sets him off. And this last week or two, he's spent hours either locked in his study or going out at odd times. I can't tell if he's hiding from me or protecting me."

Tammy tightened her grip on her cup. The heat burned, but it helped her think. "We'll find out what's really going on. I promise."

Lockie blinked up at her, tail curling once around Claire's wrist as if to second the vow.

CHAPTER 28

The Christmas market pulsed with cheer. Juniper and plum threaded the air as *Deck the Halls* lifted from the carolers clustered north of the fountain.

Wally tracked one thing: David Thompson.

Thompson moved like water, smooth and deliberate. Trained. His head checked angles, gaps, reflections. Beyond caution. Spooked.

Wally hung back and blended with the crowd of puffy coats and wool scarves that filled the western side of the square. Fairy lights from the booth roofs threw shifting glints across the snow-dusted cobblestones.

David cut through the shoppers and slid into one of the narrow lanes that ran behind the stalls, where smoke from roasting nuts tangled with the richer scent of hot chocolate and mulled wine.

He turned again without warning, darting between another set of booths toward the open space near the choir, then looping back along a cross-lane that ran between the next rows.

No pattern.

No destination.

Shaking a tail?

Wally paused at a rack of carved ornaments, pretending to study a painted reindeer. From his peripheral vision, he tracked David scanning the shoppers behind him. The man's jaw locked. Fear, maybe, or calculation.

Movement snagged Wally's attention. A figure in a dark parka and knitted cap weaved through the crowd, eyes fixed on Thompson's back. The guy moved wrong. Too obvious. Too clumsy. Not trained.

Wally's gut twisted. He glanced at David, now weaving through the next lane, slipping in and out of sight as he used the short cross-rows to change direction, then back at the amateur tail.

He yanked his phone from his pocket and hit Tammy's number.

One ring, two.

"Did you find something?"

"I've got a situation. I'm tailing David, but there's someone else on his trail. I need you to take over surveillance while I check out this new player."

"Another tail?"

"Maybe our Mr. One. They're definitely not a pro and they're young. I'm going to see what I can find out."

"Got it. Where's David headed?"

"He's circling the west side of the fountain, working the back passages. He could break in any direction. Be careful. David's got instincts."

"He's ex-law enforcement, but Claire didn't say which branch."

"This is real. Keep your distance and don't engage."

"Don't worry. I've been practicing my sneaky skills. Lockie and I will blend right in."

He ended the call and scanned for the stranger. The dark coat flashed between booths, slipping into the first back passage.

Wally followed, boots silent on powder. The carolers' chorus mixed with the deeper brass notes of the band. Adrenaline sharpened his focus.

Who was this person? Why the interest in David? Did they connect to Morton's murder? Or Henry's?

Wally closed the distance. Right now, he needed answers from the amateur skulking through the market.

The stranger disappeared into a cross-lane between a booth selling wooden toys and one brandishing knitted scarves. Wally reached the opening and peered in.

Deck the Halls rolled to a jaunty finish as he slipped into the shadows.

Joy to the World carried through the air as Tammy trailed David through the west market section.

Lockie wove around her ankles. She almost hummed, caught herself, and raised her scarf to her mouth.

Children squealed as snowballs flew. Parents juggled steaming drinks and armfuls of presents. Rosy-cheeked shoppers laughed and chatted.

David pivoted hard into a back passage by the fountain-facing stalls.

Tammy tucked beside a booth selling carved wooden ornaments and pressed close to the frame. From a distance, he looked relaxed, but his eyes kept sweeping, the restless scan of a man trained to stay on guard.

He's running from someone.

The question was who.

David vanished around the corner.

Tammy eased along the shadowed lanes, the heat from nearby cooktops brushing her face as a vendor's ladle clanked on a pot. Boots crunched. Voices rose and fell in cheerful waves.

Lockie stopped. His ears swiveled toward a gap ahead, every whisker forward.

"What is it?" she whispered.

He flicked his tail, intent. He had something.

Tammy scooped him inside her coat and pressed against the canvas back.

She edged close enough to see his back, phone clamped to his ear, shoulders bunched, free hand fisted.

She needed to call Wally, but moving now would expose her.

She eased away from the edge and scanned for the amateur tail Wally had mentioned. Faces blurred, motion everywhere. No one stood out.

Lockie's claws pricked through her sweater. He stared past her shoulder into the crowd.

Wally shadowed the stranger following David. The man lingered too long at counters lined with trinkets, pausing in clear sightlines.

They wove through the side lanes, lights flickering between gaps.

Wally lifted his phone and caught a three-quarter frame at one of the displays. Scarf up, sharp cheekbones, on the lookout. Good enough.

He hit Stanton's number.

"Male tailing David Thompson through the market. Late thirties, dark parka, gray scarf, chewing gum. Sending photo. David knows how to shake a shadow. This one does not."

"Location?"

"He's west of the fountain. Just passed the cider van and is now moving toward the coffee cart beside the candles. David's looping through the back passages behind the vendors."

"Photo received. Brown is two minutes out. Wait for backup."

"Eyes only," Wally replied, sliding with the crowd.

Steam from the cart rose sweet and thin. David paused there, nodded to the barista, then drifted sideways, killing time and checking mirrors. Old habits. Wally recognized the rhythm and gave him room.

The stranger lingered at a table of soaps and smelled a bar without sniffing it. His gaze never left David's back.

Wally let a family with strollers pass in front of him, then slid to the edge of the stall line. He caught a side angle as the stranger adjusted his scarf. Another shot. Clearer. He sent that one too.

Wally's phone buzzed. "Brown is on the southwest corner," Stanton said. "Running ID now. Hold position."

"Copy."

David did his second check. He bent to tie a boot lace near the planter, used the chrome trim to catch a reflection, then rose and changed direction by ten degrees. Smooth. The amateur missed the tell and hurried to close the distance.

Wally matched the stranger's pace from thirty feet. The market lights hummed. Music shifted; *O Come, All Ye Faithful* began, the tune rolling through the winter air. Scent from the caffeine cart kept him sharp.

His pocket thrummed. A text from Stanton: "Brown has your guy in sight from the west. Running second image now."

Wally caught himself smiling. Two angles helped. He kept the man centered and watched David slip out of the market toward the tight lane between Pizza Pasta Palooza and Mrs. Hubbard's Cupboard.

Do not run, son. Not today.

The stranger followed, pushing through the cider van line before disappearing into the shadows beyond the market.

The carolers reached their final chorus, applause rippling through the crowd and fading as he snuck into the lane.

He waited for Stanton's next ping to give him a name.

Tammy sighed a small cloud. "Right. Observe. No engaging. No—"

"Excuse me, miss?" A little boy tugged her sleeve. "Can you help me find my mom?"

She flicked between him and David, then back at the child's tear-filled cheeks. "Oh, sweetie," she said, kneeling. "Of course I will."

She'd momentarily lost sight of her target, but she couldn't abandon a lost child.

Some detective I am. Wally's going to kill me.

Lockie sauntered up, his new bell collar tinkling.

"Can you find this little guy's mom?"

He meowed, tail high, and headed off.

From behind them, *God Rest Ye Merry, Gentlemen* struck, brisk and bright, the rhythm carrying over the hum of the shoppers. The tune tangled with the sizzle of caramel popcorn and the sugary warmth drifting from the fudge stand.

They followed through the crowd until the boy shouted, "There!"—a frantic woman waving from beside the cider van.

Mother and son collided in a hug. "Nice work," she whispered into Lockie's fur. "Treats later."

She turned back to the flow of shoppers and felt her stomach drop. David was gone.

A shine of silver caught her attention in a glossy bauble. Behind her, a man in a dark coat stood very still, scarf high, watching her instead of browsing.

Smelly Peppermint Mr. One?

Her pulse ticked hard. "Lockie, I think we inherited a tail."

His fur lifted along his spine. He gave a small, steady growl.

"Okay," she said. "We will not be interesting." She drifted toward the Christmas tree, its boughs unlit, ribbons tied in loose bows.

Beside it, an ornament seller's tables shimmered, with hanging rows of blown glass catching lamplight and throwing back tiny, warped copies of her face.

Carol's pulsed behind her.

"O tidings of comfort and joy…"

She stopped within reach of the display, the reflections shifting as she moved. Red, gold, and a darker shape at her back. He was still there.

Tammy edged to the far side of the tree's lower branches. Needles brushed her coat; the bulbs clinked, a gleeful warning. Lockie's bell answered from somewhere inside the tree, faint but steady.

A shadow crossed.

He stood close now. "Ms. Rumbelow. I am Agent Rossi. We need to talk."

Agent. Thomas wasn't joking.

"As in FBI?" she blurted, trying to buy time.

Wait. Wally said he was untrained.

Rossi's lips thinned. "I'm here to make sure… delicate matters remain undisturbed. Your little investigation is treading on thin ice."

"Investigation?" Tammy let out a quick, too-bright laugh, fingers worrying a strand of hair into a rope. "I'm just a mystery writer looking for inspiration. Small town, Christmas spirit, you know the drill."

"Spare me." He didn't blink.

Heat pricked Tammy's skin. "Did I see you in Willowcroft Cemetery about five days ago? Driving a beat-up Toyota?"

His hand paused on his pocket; a muscle jumped in his jaw. He swallowed, then smoothed his expression. "You have been asking about protected witnesses."

WITSEC is run by marshals, not agents.

Lockie's eyes flashed green between the boughs.

"You and your friends are making things difficult," Rossi said. "Leave it alone."

"We should talk to the sheriff. He can—"

"No." His hand shifted inside his coat. He lunged forward.

A black-and-white streak erupted from deep within the Christmas tree. Branches wobbled; bulbs popped free; a rain of ornaments came down with him. Lockie hit the man square in the chest, yowling, claws raking, scattering glass in every direction.

"Lockie, no!"

Rossi wrenched the cat off his jacket and stumbled back, boots skidding on shards. Lockie landed lightly, sprang up again, and arched into a hiss, keeping himself between Tammy and the attacker.

"Not so fast," a voice barked.

Wally crashed into Rossi from behind. Man and cat drove him sideways through the edge of the ornament stall and straight into the gingerbread house beside it. Frosted walls and candy windows exploded into powder and shards.

Rossi twisted. Wally held, teeth clenched.

Lockie, still bristling, emerged from the wreckage and perched himself on the collapsed gingerbread roof, tail flicking through a haze of sugar dust.

"A little help here?" Wally grunted, struggling to keep him down.

A second set of hands locked Rossi's wrist and rolled his shoulder. David. He moved like a man who had not forgotten his training.

"Hold him," Wally said.

The carolers stumbled to a stop mid-chorus. A few gasps rose, then silence fell, broken only by the clink of rolling decorations across the cobbles.

Sheriff Stanton burst onto the scene. Lamby trotted at his side, tail high. A muscle ticked in his cheek as he took in the chaos: shattered ornaments, scattered gingerbread walls, and the suspect pinned to the stones under Wally and David.

"Well, well." The sheriff unclipped his handcuffs. "Christmas has come early for the department."

Rossi's glare sliced toward Tammy. "This is not over." He spat a wad of gum.

"It is for today." Stanton secured the cuffs shut with a metallic click and began reading him his rights.

Lamby trotted closer, sniffing the air around the man's boots. He paused over the gum, gave a tentative sniff, then sneezed once. A short pause followed before two quicker sneezes burst out, sharp and certain.

Stanton's brow furrowed. His gaze dropped to the gum, then flicked briefly to Lamby and back to the assailant. "You again." He pulled an evidence bag from his pocket and collected the gum, recognition plain in his expression. "Oaktown."

Tammy caught the word. Definitely number one.

Lockie hopped down from his perch and padded over to Lamby.

Feline cool met canine duty in a brief standoff worthy of a Western.

Lamby wagged once; Lockie's whiskers twitched, then came the soft rumble of acceptance.

Partnership sealed.

Tammy scooped Lockie up and pressed a kiss on his head. "Double treats for you, Pawlock Holmes."

Lamby huffed, the sound somewhere between a sneeze and a laugh, as if in agreement.

The sheriff patted Lamby on the head. "Treats for you too later."

"What did Lamby do?" asked Tammy.

Stanton rubbed Lamby's ears. "He'd never been a sneezy dog until the State Park crime scene. Then it happened again a couple of times in

Oaktown. First when this guy barreled into us, and second with Olivia's peppermint mocha." He raised his head. "I thought Lamby was getting sick, so I took him to the vet."

Lamby sneezed once, then twice more.

"The vet asked me to list when it started and every other time and place it happened. If she hadn't asked, I might've missed it. I initially blamed the mint, but if that was the culprit, he'd be sneezing constantly since it's everywhere right now."

Lockie sneezed. Tammy glared at him. *Was that a sympathy sneeze?*

"That's when it clicked. We found gum at Morton's crime scene. I had multiple witnesses mention a gum-chewing guy during our investigation."

Stanton pointed to Rossi. "This guy is always chewing gum, including in Oaktown. At first, I was stumped by Olivia's mocha, then I remembered I picked up a gum wrapper off the floor dropped by him. So Lamby was reacting to that rather than her drink."

He held up an evidence bag with a wad inside. "Turns out there's an ingredient in gum some dogs are allergic to, and Lamby is one of them. Now we have a wad from this scene to compare with the one found in the State Park. That should nail this guy."

David pulled the sheriff away. The sheriff's expression turned thoughtful when David murmured something low. Behind them, Brown collected a scarf and a wallet that had slid free.

"Nothing to see here, folks!" Wally called out, dusting snow from his jacket. "Just some good old-fashioned Christmas hijinks!"

The carolers rallied with a peppy *Rudolph the Red-Nosed Reindeer*. The noise of the market returned in a wave, as if nothing had happened.

Tammy let herself be carried away by the music. Flurries appeared, coating the mess at their feet.

She glanced at David and the sheriff, heads bent, voices too low to carry. Her writer's instinct pricked. There was more to that exchange than a simple arrest.

"Do you want to know what that's about?" Wally asked, gesturing toward the two men. "Thompson's a retired U.S. marshal. WITSEC branch."

CHAPTER 29

Tammy slipped through the disguised bookshelf door and let it click softly back into place. The scent of cinnamon tea wrapped around her, but it did little to thaw the cold that had settled in her chest.

Olivia, Mrs. T, and Xander sat at the table, notes spread between them, mid-conversation. The moment they saw her face, everything stopped.

Olivia set down her pen. "What happened?"

Tammy tried to sound calm, fingers tightening on the back of a chair. "There was... an incident at the market."

Mrs. T rose halfway from her chair. "Are you hurt?"

"I'm fine. Thanks to Wally and David." She pulled in a breath. "Mr. One from our suspects list confronted me. He said he was Agent Rossi. He wanted me to stop investigating. When I called his bluff, he went for me."

Olivia's hand flew to her mouth. "He attacked you?"

"Lockie launched at him first. Wally tackled him. David helped pin him down."

Mrs. T pressed a hand to her chest. "Good heavens."

"Stanton showed up right after. He arrested the guy. Wally stayed behind with David to sort out the details."

Xander sat forward. "Remember when the internet went wonky?"

"You mean the aliens?" Tammy dropped into an empty chair.

Xander tapped his keyboard. "And a federal case."

"I was distracted by the red-velvet cake." Mrs. T resumed knitting.

"And the frosting," said Olivia.

Xander kept typing. "What if I search Agent Rossi plus federal cases plus 1995?"

"You think it was connected after all?" Mrs. T asked.

Xander stopped scrolling. "Here. A drug trafficking case, 1995. Federal involvement. Marshals, DEA, the whole alphabet soup."

He used the name to intimidate me, thinking I'd know what it meant. Tammy gripped the edge of the table. I'm glad I didn't.

Olivia's expression hardened. "A Rossi *senior*, I'm assuming, was the accused because if you're talking about the rude man I met in the candy store, he wasn't old enough to be doing anything criminal thirty years ago."

Mrs. T's knitting needles stilled. "Impersonating a federal agent is a serious crime."

Lockie jumped up, curling neatly beside a stack of notes. His whiskers twitched. He gave a soft approving chuff, as if confirming they were on the right scent.

"Wally said David was a Witness Protection marshal."

Olivia tossed her pen. "He was our best suspect—oops."

Xander glanced up from the screen. "If that name came from an old federal case, maybe it ties back to whatever David's been keeping quiet about."

Tammy's gaze drifted to Lockie, his eyes half-closed but alert. "Rossi said I'd been asking about protected witnesses. Does that mean the Winters at the inn were in WITSEC even though Deputy Brown's dad said no one claimed them?"

Mrs. T pursed her lips. "We'll never hear the end of it once Georgina finds out she's been part of Witness Protection."

Olivia groaned. "Do you think George knew?"

"Hard to say," Mrs. T said. "He's always been tight-lipped. Maybe he had his reasons."

Xander scooted his chair closer to the table. "You think there were others? People hidden here under new names?"

Mrs. T gave a small shrug. "In Willowcroft? Stranger things have happened, dear."

"What was the outcome of the 1995 case?" asked Tammy.

Xander skimmed his screen. "The federal case was dropped after the prosecution lost key witnesses, leaving them with not enough evidence to proceed, but was found guilty of lesser state charges."

"Does it say what happened to the witnesses?" asked Olivia.

Xander searched more. "They died in a car crash in Iowa a month before the trial."

CHAPTER 30

"Special Agent Rodriguez with the FBI." The man extended his credentials to Wally along with his hand.

Wally shook it, studying the agent's face as he slid into the booth. Outside, fat snowflakes drifted past the diner windows. Stanton settled beside the agent.

Peggy swept past in a storm of red velvet and jingling bells. The apron stretched across her frame bore an embroidered reindeer mid-leap, its nose a pom-pom that swayed with every step. Her glasses frames were wrapped in tiny candy-cane stripes.

She laid down three mugs and poured coffee. "What'll it be, gentlemen?"

Wally leaned back against the vinyl seatback. The Swinging Spoon's lunch rush hummed around him, a blur of clattering dishes and conversation.

"I'll try the gingerbread pancakes. Everyone swears they're life-changing."

"Best thing on the Christmas menu," Peggy confirmed. "Whipped cream?"

"Extra."

She turned to the man across from him. "And you, stranger?"

"Just the coffee." The newcomer's words carried the clipped weight of authority.

Peggy raised an eyebrow. "You must be the out-of-towner. Sheriff said we had a guest."

"Guilty. Only been in town a few days."

Days. Before or after Morton's death? Stanton's been keeping secrets.

"Then welcome to Willowcroft." She turned to the sheriff.

"Pot roast. But you already knew that."

She winked. "Habit's hard to break."

Peggy's reindeer apron swayed as she spun toward the kitchen.

Wally's phone sat face-down beside the plastic snowman centerpiece. He flipped it over, then looked from Stanton to Rodriguez.

"I want my team in on this. They've earned it."

The agent's jaw tightened. His fingers drummed once against the table-top.

Stanton waved a hand. "Wally's team is solid. I'll vouch for them."

Rodriguez hesitated. "Keep it private."

"They know how."

The agent relented with a sigh. "Fine, but no amateur-sleuth blogging."

Wally tapped Tammy's number and hit the speaker icon. The line rang twice before she answered.

"Hold on." A shuffling sound, then, "Okay, we're all here. You're on speaker."

The agent shifted in his seat, one hand dragging down his face.

Wally had been waiting for this conversation ever since David made his tail and confronted him in one smooth move—revealing he was a marshal while calling out Wally's rusty surveillance skills. Now, maybe, he'd get the full story.

Rodriguez tapped a knuckle against the Formica. "An archive clerk accessing a 1995 file triggered our warning system. It was a case no one was ever sure was truly closed, hence the trace. I spoke with the now-unemployed clerk, and he admitted sending Rossi to Willowcroft. So here I am."

Wally paused mid-coffee sip. The noise of the diner dimmed behind the words *warning system.*

"Two murders weren't part of my plan," Rodriguez finished.

Stanton stirred the sugar in his coffee. "At least he caved fast."

"The arrested man is Antonio Rossi Junior from Chicago. His father would be mortified at how quickly he confessed."

"Too right." Stanton set down his spoon.

"The son's no criminal mastermind. He grew up nursing the lie that his father was the victim, not the perpetrator. Rossi Senior told his son the government ruined his life. Claimed the witnesses lied and destroyed an innocent man and his family."

Peggy returned, balancing plates with the grace of long practice. She set Wally's gingerbread pancakes before him, the delectable cream piled high with a dusting of cinnamon on top. Stanton's pot roast landed next.

"Anything else?"

"We're good." Wally smiled up at her.

She lingered a heartbeat too long before moving away.

Stanton worked his fork through his pot roast. "Morton was hired to find the ruby. He was told the main suspects were a Winters family staying at Willowcroft Inn the night of a blizzard in 1995. The family vanished in the middle of the night, and the necklace was discovered missing the following day."

"That's not a lot to go on after thirty years." Rodriguez hooked a finger through the handle and drew his mug closer.

"Morton kept meticulous records we were able to access from his laptop found in his hotel room." The sheriff took a bite.

Wally gave Stanton a stern look. "Did you now?" *Thanks for the heads up—not.*

The agent picked up his coffee. "He interviewed the innkeeper and stopped at the *Gazette*."

"That's how Thomas got the idea to write the 'Remember When' article," said Stanton. "He used the feature as cover to question Brown and me and to funnel information back to Morton. I spoke with him earlier to confirm the PI had been to see him, but he clammed up."

"He takes the paper seriously," said Wally.

"He confirmed it later. Claimed he was protecting a source. Turns out *he* was the source."

Wally cut into his pancakes. "Did they see Sheriff Brown's notes about witness protection?"

"Potentially," admitted Stanton.

Rodriguez rotated his cup between his palms. "But it would be an easy leap for Morton after not finding a Winters family aside from death notices years earlier. That's the perfect setup for an alias, official or otherwise. His laptop also showed recently used object-recognition software, basically the same idea as facial recognition but for objects."

"Xander used the same method, and we got a copy of the exact photo in Morton's hand."

"Did he now?" Stanton glared at Wally.

The agent also shot Wally a look, but a more complimentary one. "Good work. Of all places to give yourself away, a Florida art gallery opening."

"It only took one phone call to request a copy of a supposedly random photo from years ago that no one should have cared about." Wally scooped up a spoonful of spiced cream.

The diner's front door swung open, and a group of carolers spilled inside, their cheeks flushed from the cold. They clustered near the counter, laughing and chattering as they shed their scarves. One of them hummed *Winter Wonderland*.

"But why did the clerk access the file that got Junior involved?" Tammy's words crackled over the speaker.

"Well, that's the thing. The photo proved the necklace was still out there but did not reveal who the person was, so Morton had to go back to the witness theory. He bribed a friend's contact, the ex-clerk, who happily took cash for access to closed documents that were often useful in insurance-fraud checks."

"What sort of information did it contain?" Tammy asked.

"Case numbers, time stamps, and supervising districts, but nothing that would have led Morton anywhere."

"So it was a dead end," said Wally.

Rodriguez cupped his mug. "As far as Morton was concerned, yes. But that request triggered Rossi's involvement."

"And two deaths." Stanton wiped his mouth.

"The clerk spotted a code in the document that tied to the year and district of Senior's failed prosecution. The man—a fixer who played both sides of the law and knew Junior—saw an opportunity to cash in twice. He tipped Junior that someone was digging into his father's case, mentioning that a PI was looking for links to a Michigan town called Willowcroft."

"So Rossi comes to Willowcroft." Olivia joined the conversation.

"The family was lucky they left when they did back in '95. The Rossis had learned the witnesses were here. When the family 'died' in a car crash, the federal case collapsed. But Senior never accepted the story. He convinced his son the government was shielding the real criminals who could prove his innocence."

"So Junior comes to town to find out what Morton knows." Tammy again.

"He booked a room at the Oaktown Inn where Morton was staying and followed him, including to a meeting with Henry Beaumont."

"Things soured fast," Stanton said. "Rossi confronted Morton, who maintained he was just chasing the necklace for Henry. The interrogation spiraled, and Morton ended up dead."

"Then he went after Henry." Olivia's voice tightened.

Peggy approached them again, pot in hand. Her smile looked strained, her movements jerky. She refilled Rodriguez's cup without asking, the stream of coffee wavering. A few drops splashed onto the table. "Everything okay here?"

"Fine," Stanton replied.

She left, but her hand trembled as she walked away. Wally caught the way her fingers gripped the handle, knuckles white.

She'd been close enough to overhear.

"Poor Henry was only trying to recover a family heirloom," said Stanton.

Rodriguez took a sip of his fresh coffee. "He had no idea what he had started and had nothing useful for Junior, so Junior killed him, believing he was part of the cover-up."

"And then he came after me." Tammy came through low on the line.

Wally could picture them in the bookstore, gathered around the phone. Xander with his arms crossed, Mrs. T's hand pressed to her chest, Olivia close to Tammy.

"He assumed you were the next layer of handlers hiding the witnesses. He called himself Agent Rossi to either make you back off or see if you'd share information."

"For some reason, he also admitted to stealing the town Santa suit," said a puzzled Stanton. "Mrs. Peters had informed me she found it, but minus the hat. So I asked him where it was, and he swore there hadn't been one."

"Mike saw Santa trying to break into the bookstore. He was coming after us. Me." Olivia's breath hitched over the speaker.

"Thank goodness Mike scared him off." Mrs. T joined the chorus, followed by a muffled, "I wonder where the hat is?"

The agent shook his head at the speaker interlopers. "Rossi said he was looking for any files Morton might've shared. He thought if he scared you enough, you'd expose the family."

The carolers at the counter launched into *Deck the Halls,* their notes rising in harmony. A few diners clapped along, and someone at the back booth whistled.

"I still don't quite get it," said Tammy.

"Junior believed Morton and Henry were part of a new cover-up. In his mind, he framed both killings as revenge and bait," explained Rodriguez. "And a way to lure the real witnesses out."

Wally released a slow sigh. "All built on a lie his father told him."

"Exactly. The old files still list the witness family as deceased in a car crash. It was considered suspect but believable enough to close the case. But all of this has reopened the question. Only David Thompson knows what really happened the night of the blizzard."

Wally set down his fork. "So the family's been alive all along, and David's kept their whereabouts to himself."

"That's where we stand. The case against Senior is closed. Junior confessed, and DNA on peppermint gum supports it." He paused. "The threat's gone, but the truth about the 'Winters' family is something David will have to explain. And believe me, he will be dealt with. He and Claire are under federal orders to remain in town until we sort it all out."

"We've got them rooms at the Willowcroft Inn," said Stanton. "Georgina will keep us informed of any developments."

Snickers came through the speaker, followed by a faint, "I bet she will. She'll know every move they make."

"Now, now." Stanton addressed the phone. "She's showing the meaning of being a model citizen."

Wally considered his town, the tunnels beneath it, and the secrets they held that destroyed multiple families. Now Morton, a PI who'd just been doing his job; Henry Beaumont, a man chasing an heirloom; and the Winters family, whoever they were and wherever they'd been hiding, waiting for the day they could stop running.

Peggy returned, this time without the coffee pot. She set the check on the table, her hand steadier now. "Take your time."

"Thanks, Peggy."

She paused, tray tucked to her side, and angled closer to the booth. "I didn't mean to eavesdrop. But if there's a family out there who can finally come home, I think that's the best Christmas gift anyone could ask for."

Wally met her gaze. The warmth in her eyes was as steady as the glow from the diner tree. "I think so too."

She walked away, and the bells on her shoes tinkled.

Stanton reached for the check, but Rodriguez beat him to it. "Bureau's buying."

"Good." Stanton pushed his empty plate aside. "Because I'm not expensing gingerbread pancakes."

Wally smiled, the first real one since the conversation started.

He ended the call and slipped the phone into his pocket. Across the table, the agent drained his coffee, and Stanton left a generous tip. The carolers concluded their song, and the diner erupted in applause.

Wally stood. The snow outside had thickened, blanketing the street in white.

Rodriguez buttoned his coat and turned toward the door. Stanton followed, pausing to wave at Peggy. She waved back.

Wally took one last look at the diner, at the families, couples, and lone diners scattered throughout. At the festive centerpiece and the gingerbread pancakes he hadn't finished. And at Peggy, refilling a customer's mug, her candy-cane glasses glinting in the light.

Then he stepped outside, into the cold and the quiet.

Next door, Olivia's windows glowed. His team was waiting.

Chapter 31

The bell above the bookstore door jingled.

Heavy footsteps navigated through the stacks, deliberate and unhurried. The hidden bookcase door yawned open.

Conversation died.

Olivia gestured toward their guests, her hand making a little flourish she hadn't intended. "Look who came for a visit."

David Thompson hunched over the worktable, hands braced on the edge. Fatigue carved deep grooves into his face. Claire anchored herself beside him, spine straight, mouth in a determined line. Mrs. T and Xander had abandoned their notebooks and drinks.

Wally eased the door closed. "Didn't expect to see you here so soon."

David swallowed hard. His eyes traveled across the group. "I figured it was time. You've earned the truth."

Claire whirled toward him. "What truth?"

He steadied himself with a breath. "Thirty years ago, I was a U.S. marshal. My assignment was the Winters family."

"A marshal?" Claire's pitch rose sharply. "You...David, why wouldn't you ever...?"

"Because I wasn't supposed to tell anyone." His words scraped low, rough as sandpaper. "The Winters were key witnesses in a federal case against a man named Rossi. I got word the family had been compromised. And then came the blizzard."

Tammy scooted closer. "You used it as cover?"

He acknowledged with a head dip. "We'd run out of options. Roads were closing. If they vanished that night, everyone, especially the Rossi family, would believe it. So I staged an accident."

Plot twist.

"I picked them up. We drove south to get out of the blizzard's path and set the scene to look like a vehicle forced into a snowdrift and into a tree." He rubbed his palms, as if warming old fingers. "The family posed while I took photos that would identify them but not the vehicle."

This is straight out of a movie.

"I got them somewhere safe out of the storm, then found a truck-stop one-hour photo along I-80 and developed the film. I faxed the images to an old college friend, a reporter desperate for a break. I told him to run it as if it happened near him in Iowa. It became the scoop of his career, a federal witness tragedy."

The picture was terrible and perfect. Olivia sucked her top lip into her bottom one. *He'd made ghosts to keep a family alive.*

"My friend told himself it was a white lie for a good cause. I told myself I was keeping the Winters alive."

Heat crept up Olivia's neck as the pieces marinated together. "That's why the case was dropped."

David nodded. "With the witnesses presumed dead, there was no testimony and the file was sealed. Officially, the Winters family died that night. Unofficially..." He stared at the floor. "I managed them under new names for as long as I could. It wasn't standard procedure. I thought giving them freedom meant safety."

Claire's fingers tangled and untangled. "And all this time, you never told me."

He met her look. Guilt etched his features. "I wanted to. Every day. But the fewer who knew, the safer you were."

She pressed a hand to her mouth. A sharp, humorless laugh followed. "The alarms, the cameras, the way you'd flinch when headlights passed the house... I called you cautious."

"I was. For both of us."

Tammy wrapped her arms across her chest. "When did the past catch up?"

"A week ago. A contact from D.C. reached out. Someone had accessed a relocation file... mine. I knew it could lead back to the staged crash. Claire had booked the market, and canceling would've raised flags. I hadn't been to Willowcroft since '95, and I wanted to see it again before bringing Claire, in case I gave something away. I stayed in Oaktown instead of at the inn."

He dragged his palm over his stubble. "That's when I spotted Rossi Junior." His jaw tensed. "I'd kept tabs on him for years. I knew his face, his temper. When he showed up here, I knew something bad was about to happen. I started tailing him and discovered he was following Morton."

Mrs. T's knitting lay neglected in her lap. "So you were following the follower."

"I overheard Morton asking around the market about a ruby. It meant nothing to me. But then he asked about the family at the inn. That's when Rossi reacted. The necklace didn't interest him either—but the family did. That told me the danger wasn't random. Whatever Junior wanted, it was tied to the Winters, not a piece of jewelry."

Olivia's curiosity simmered.

"They didn't know anyone in town," David continued, "let alone anything about a necklace. It had to be a coincidence."

Wally shook his head. "I don't believe in those, as I'm sure you don't."

David shrugged.

"Morton stumbled into something without understanding it," said Tammy.

"He slipped Rossi in the market, I caught him by the elbow and tried to warn him, but he wouldn't listen. There was a struggle, and he stormed off."

Confusion crossed Tammy's face. "The yarn..."

Olivia straightened, bouncing slightly on her toes despite sitting. "That's how it got there. From Claire's stock to David's sleeve, then to Morton's crime scene."

David's words roughened, fraying at the edges. "You found Morton's body the next day. I'd lost Junior while warning Morton. I should have stayed with him; at least then I might have been able to intervene when things went down."

He exhaled shakily and looked at Claire.

He blames himself.

Mrs. T sat forward. "So when you helped Wally with the arrest—"

"I knew Junior and what he'd most likely done."

David turned to the murder board. He approached and extracted the Winters family photo. "Where did you get this?"

"I found it on the ground at the market," Tammy said.

He gave a weary dip of his head. "I didn't mean for it to end up in anyone's hands. At least yours were a better option than Rossi's."

Tammy blinked. "You dropped the photo?"

David's shoulders sagged. "The night I heard my file had been accessed, I pulled my old field box from storage to make sure my memory wasn't playing tricks. While I sorted through the paperwork, an old photograph fell loose—a picture that the Winters girl had mailed me years after they disappeared. It came with a thank-you note, no return address."

He paused. "Claire walked in. I tucked it into my wallet before she could see what I was holding. I forgot about it afterward. I didn't realize I'd lost it until now. It must have fallen out."

Wally planted his palms on the table. "You've done a hell of a job keeping ghosts hidden, David. But can't they come out now?"

"Yes. Junior has confessed to two murders, so he'll be locked up for the rest of his life. I can tell the family it's over."

He produced a black satellite phone from his pocket, old, scuffed, but clearly cared for.

Claire's breath hitched. "David, you can't—"

"I can. They've lived like shadows because of me. They deserve better."

He keyed in a long string of numbers. Everyone watched. Lockie sprang onto the table, tail flicking.

This is it. A hard knock of pulse hit, then another. *Thirty years simmering, about to boil over.*

Several rings came through the speaker. Then—click.

"Hello?" A woman answered.

David's throat tightened. "Hailey? It's... it's David."

The silence shattered into a gasp. "David?"

"It's me. You're safe, I hope?"

"We're okay." Her words quivered. "But I don't understand. What's happened? Do we have to move again?"

Tears threatened. Olivia mashed her knuckles against her lips.

"No. The danger's over. Junior's gone now too. You can come home."

"Home?" Her voice broke. "Can I go to Willowcroft?"

"If that's what you want." Moisture gathered at his lashes. "It's Christmas, Hailey. You've been running long enough."

Olivia's curiosity bubbled over. She scrawled a note, her handwriting more frantic than usual, and slid it toward him: *Ask her if she's Gwendolyn.*

David pulled a face but asked the question.

Nothing came back.

"How do you know that name?"

"I'm not alone. I'm with people from Willowcroft who have been looking for you."

Mrs. T interrupted. "Hailey, dear, if you are Gwendolyn, we have the letters you wrote to Jeremiah. But no one knows who Jeremiah is."

"Did none of my letters get through?"

She is Gwendolyn.

"I'm sorry, dear, but no. We'd be happy to deliver them if you tell us who he is?"

A small sound escaped her, part sob, part laugh. "I never knew his real name. We were to meet in the cemetery that night you moved us, David. I wanted to explain, but you wouldn't let me go."

Mrs. T gasped.

Cemetery! Olivia's stomach lurched, a recipe with the final ingredient just dropped in.

"He waited for me, didn't he?" Hailey's words trembled.

"Yes, dear. His name is Archie."

"Archie?"

"He was out in the storm all night and nearly got frostbite. He never told anyone why he was at the cemetery during a blizzard. He's hated Christmas ever since. I think he's been waiting for you."

A long pause, then Hailey whispered, "Do you really think so?"

Tammy smiled faintly. "I think he'll be very glad to see you."

"I never forgot him. Not once."

"We can tell from your letters. Come home for Christmas, Hailey."

Static rushed the line, then a shaky breath. "I'm on my way."

When the call ended, David deflated. Claire reached for him, her fingers unsteady.

Olivia's vision blurred. A blush crept up her neck from the delicious weight of it all. A love story marinating for three decades, finally ready to serve.

Tammy swiped a tear from her cheek.

Lockie gave a small chirp and rubbed David's leg.

Chapter 32

"She's really coming?" Olivia's knuckles whitened around the edge of the table.

The back room of Bookworm Haven smelled of stale coffee, pepperoni, and onions, the lingering aftermath of an all-night debrief. Tammy had her cheek pillowed on folded arms, eyelids dragging with each blink. Wally stood by the window, one palm flat against the cold glass, tracking snowflakes as they spiraled down. Mrs. T's needles clicked on, steady as a metronome.

Tammy lifted her head and stretched. "David confirmed her flight lands in Detroit this afternoon. He'll meet her and drive her to town. But...not everyone in Willowcroft is going to greet her with chocolates and carols."

"You mean the ones who think the Winters stole the Beaumont ruby," said Mrs. T.

Wally pushed away from the window and scraped a hand through his hair. "I can talk to Thomas at the *Gazette.* He'll print the truth about witness protection, federal cover-up, the whole bit." He braced both hands on the table. "But it won't be out before she arrives."

"Then she'll walk into a storm," Tammy said.

Mrs. T's needles stilled. "Not if we get ahead of it."

Olivia frowned. "How?"

"With the oldest weapon in town. Gossip."

Tammy blinked. "You mean fight rumors with... rumors?"

"Precisely." Mrs. T put away her knitting. "If the story's going to spread, we might as well choose the correct version."

Wally groaned. "I'm not sure I like where this is heading."

"You don't have to." Mrs. T pushed to her feet in one smooth motion. "Just trust me. Leave this to the Willow Crafters. You prepare Archie and we'll ready Willowcroft for Hailey."

Olivia exchanged a wary look with Tammy. "That sounds slightly ominous."

"On the contrary, dear." Mrs. T retrieved her coat and knitting bag. "It sounds effective."

Flurries fell in lazy spirals over Founders Row, dusting the wrought-iron gates of the Beaumont estate.

Olivia's boots crunched through fresh powder as she trekked the drive with Tammy and Wally. The grand old house loomed ahead, equal parts grandeur and gloom. The murders were solved, but exhaustion clung to her bones. Still, work remained.

"Our last conversation didn't go very well," Wally said.

Tammy pulled her scarf tighter. "Thirty years is a long time to carry bitterness. We tread gently."

Inside, they crossed faded parquet beneath crystal chandeliers that had witnessed generations of Beaumonts. Cedar polish hung in the air, mingling with the mustiness of antique leather-bound books that no one had cracked open and silver that demanded constant care to stay bright.

Christmas had tiptoed in. Garlands draped the banister without conviction. Unopened boxes of ornaments lay stacked by the fireplace. Marion Beaumont sat by the window in her wheelchair, thin hands folded in her lap. A wool blanket covered her knees. Pearls glinted at her throat.

She looked up as the trio entered but remained silent.

Across the room, Archie Beaumont stood at the mantel, already scowling. "If this is about the past, I've done my best to forget it."

Tammy glanced at Olivia. "It hasn't forgotten you."

Marion drew back. "What are they talking about, Archie?"

"I'm not sure, Mother."

Olivia moved closer. "We found Gwendolyn."

Archie went still. His fingers clamped on the mantelpiece edge. The fire hissed. Nothing else. "Don't—Don't use that name."

Marion's forehead creased. She searched each face. "Gwendolyn Beaumont Lund died nearly a hundred years ago. What are you going on about?"

"Her real name is Hailey." Olivia kept her tone steady. "She was in WITSEC because her father was involved in a federal case in 1995. She didn't leave you by choice."

Archie spun around. Disbelief fought something older, more fragile. "Witness protection? That's—no. No, she left."

Wally's words were quiet but carried weight. "She was *moved* fast. She wasn't allowed to say goodbye."

Archie dragged a hand across the back of his neck. "All these years, I thought..." He stopped. His Adam's apple bobbed. "I thought she didn't love me enough."

"Would someone please tell me what is going on?" Marion's plea cut through the room.

Archie didn't turn. Tammy continued. "She wrote to you every Christmas for thirty years. Mr. Taylor has the letters at the post office."

"She wrote... all this time?"

"Every single year." Olivia let that sink in. "She never stopped hoping you were out there thinking of her."

The fire crackled in the quiet.

Marion reached for her son's hand.

Archie's jaw locked. He stared out the snow-dusted window.

"She's on her way home." Tammy paused. "The necklace will be here tomorrow."

Marion's fingers tightened around Archie's hand. "Did you say necklace? What do you know about that?"

No one answered.

The fire popped, sending a prickle of heat across Olivia's cheeks. Archie's fingers twitched on the mantel, Marion's question hanging unanswered. Tammy's throat bobbed. Even Wally's steady composure cracked, his attention fixed on the hearth. Olivia pressed her hands together and focused on the rug's worn weave.

Marion scanned their faces. "Who has it?" The words came sharp, high. "How did you three find it when the private investigator couldn't?"

Olivia's mouth tensed. "You knew about that?"

Marion's expression went hard. "Of course I did. I was the one who hired him."

The three exchanged quick glances. The revelation drew a cold draft through the room.

Marion lifted her chin. "I wanted the necklace back before Christmas. To wear it one more time before I died. I offered Morton a substantial bonus if he could recover it in time. I authorized him to do whatever it took, saying money was no object."

Wally shifted his weight. "We thought Henry hired him."

Marion's pearls caught the firelight as she adjusted them. "No. I barely leave the estate anymore. Cobblestones and wheelchairs don't mix. Henry met with him off the estate for me. He wanted that necklace more than Archie, so I let him handle the meetings."

Her son turned sharply. "You never told me."

"I didn't see the point. I knew you wouldn't approve."

The air between mother and son hung heavy with secrets kept too long.

Archie's shoulders slumped. The fight drained from him. "Gwendo—Hailey still has it."

Marion jerked. "You knew who had it?"

He nodded, his gaze distant. "I gave it to her."

Marion's hand fell from his sleeve as if burned. Her pearls pulled taut at her neck. "You... what?"

Archie pressed on. "The night of the storm. We were supposed to run away together. I thought the necklace would give us a fresh start, money, freedom, whatever we needed." He swallowed. "But she never came. I waited while the blizzard buried the roads and me along with them. I thought she'd tricked me. That she'd taken it and vanished."

Olivia's throat constricted. "But she didn't."

"No." Archie's whisper reached no one and everyone. "She was taken. All this time..."

Wally stepped in gently. "We're still working through the details. We'll be in touch once it's all sorted."

Archie gave a small dip of his head, testing the shape of the future. "Tomorrow." Then firmer. "Tomorrow."

Wally touched the brim of his hat. "We can see ourselves out."

They left the room to its silence, the fire's hiss, and the weight of what had been said. Outside, the front door clicked shut behind them, and cold air rushed to meet Olivia's burning face.

Tomorrow everything changes.

CHAPTER 33

Hazel imagined the statue built in their honor—five women armed with knitting needles, walkie-talkies, and the ability to weaponize small-town gossip.

Marjorie called it Operation Gossip.

"If we can't stop the rumor mill," she'd said, "we might as well turn it to our advantage."

Each Willow Crafter had her assignment, her target, and a walkie-talkie with a glittery call sign courtesy of Betty.

Marjorie insisted hers was Command.

They fanned out across town in the hope of setting off a chain reaction of gossip.

Marjorie entered Mrs. Hubbard's Cupboard loud enough to rattle the canned goods.

Her daughter-in-law, Katie, was restocking a pyramid of apples.

"You'll never guess what I've heard," Marjorie began, pitched perfectly to reach every curious ear in range.

"You remember that family I told you about who vanished from the Inn during the blizzard of '95, taking the Beaumont necklace with them?"

"Yes."

"They were innocent!"

Marjorie paused, and two shoppers drifted closer. "The necklace has been found. Entire story wrong for thirty years."

She walked out ten minutes later, pretending not to notice the whisper chain forming behind her.

She lifted her walkie-talkie. "Command to Unit Teacup. Spark ignited. Grocery sector gossiping."

Hazel crackled back. "Roger that, Command."

Hazel's mission was subtle reinforcement at Sweet Crumbs. She ordered a gingerbread man sporting a bow tie, then leaned toward Mrs. Applewood.

"Did you hear? That family from the blizzard had federal ties."

Mrs. Applewood dropped her rolling pin.

"Witness protection. The poor things had to flee that night for their safety. Imagine!"

Mrs. Applewood gasped so hard a puff of flour rose between them. "So Georgina's inn was part of a government program?"

Hazel only smiled. "I couldn't possibly say."

She keyed her walkie under the counter. "Unit Teapot to Command. Pastry sector converted. Flour flying."

Della Mae entered the Willowcroft Inn like she was carrying classified information, which, technically, she was.

"Georgina," she said solemnly, "you might want to brace yourself. You were part of a covert operation."

The innkeeper blinked. "What?"

"That strange family who disappeared thirty years ago? Witness protection. You sheltered them! Probably saved their lives."

From his armchair, George grunted without looking up. "Told you they weren't tourists."

"You knew?" Georgina shrieked.

"Need-to-know basis. You didn't."

Della Mae retreated before the argument could reach full volume. She snickered into her walkie. "Unit Button to Command. Inn detonated."

Betty never whispered when she could project. Peggy at the Swinging Spoon didn't stand a chance.

"Peggy, dearest, I just heard the most touching story! The girl from that old blizzard family. Archie Beaumont was in love with her! That's why he was in the cemetery that night."

Peggy's hand jerked. Coffee sloshed over the rim.

"The girl was in danger, swept away by Witness Protection! And Archie Beaumont, poor darling, waited in the snow for her. Frostbitten but faithful!"

Two regulars at the counter debated whether Archie's vigil counted as "the most romantic act of devotion in Michigan history." Betty hummed *All I Want for Christmas Is You* before activating her walkie. "Unit Cupcake to Command. Diner secured. Patrons swooning. Over."

Marjorie replied, dry as toast. "Try not to dramatize frostbite, Cupcake."

Beatrice sat under the dryer at Teased and Polished, its jet-engine hum filling the salon. Her hairstylist, Vanessa, leaned close while Bree buffed her nails.

"I'm only telling you all this because you're professionals."

"Oh, we're very discreet," said Vanessa, already grinning.

"The daughter's returning soon."

Bree dropped her nail file. "That explains why he never married!"

"Exactly," Beatrice said with great solemnity. "A heart that loyal can't be redirected."

Bree bounced in her chair. "This is better than Netflix!"

Within minutes, two customers with foils in their hair were repeating the story—with added details involving an engagement ring and an FBI helicopter.

Outside, Beatrice smirked into her walkie. "Unit Bluebird to Command. Salon gossip exceeds expectations. Possibly airborne and being turned into a Hallmark script."

That evening, the Willow Crafters crew gathered in Hazel's living room, walkie-talkies lined up beside their teacups.

Marjorie checked her notes. "Supermarket—secure. Bakery—converted. Diner—emotional. Inn—volatile. Salon—uncontainable."

"Georgina's demanding a federal pension," Della Mae said.

Betty laughed. "And I overheard two teenagers call the cemetery 'Lover's Bluff.'"

Hazel leaned back in her chair. "And when Hailey arrives, she'll walk into kindness instead of suspicion."

Marjorie nodded. "Operation Gossip was a complete success."

Hazel chuckled into her cup. Willowcroft's rumor mill had finally spun something worth repeating.

Betty clicked her walkie's button. "Unit Cupcake signing off—with love and justice."

The devices crackled as Marjorie sighed. "I'm confiscating those immediately."

"Not yet," Hazel said, setting her teacup down. "We've set the record straight. Now we make sure Hailey and Archie get their happy ending."

Beatrice leaned forward. "You're thinking a public reunion?"

"Private," Hazel said. "Something just for them."

Marjorie's eyes twinkled. "Leave that to me. I'm due for a final walk-through of the light trail before the unveiling. No one will question it."

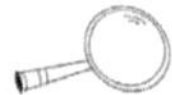

Snow drifted over Willowcroft in soft, silent flakes as the last of the afternoon light faded from the sky. The square buzzed with anticipation for that night's tree lighting, but on the edge of town, a quieter plan was unfolding.

Mrs. T stood by the entrance to the park trail, lantern in hand. "Everything ready, Marjorie?" she asked into her walkie.

"Lanterns lit and path clear," came the reply. "Archie is in place, waiting."

A car door closed in the distance. David Thompson's silhouette appeared, escorting a woman bundled in a deep blue coat. Even through the flurries, Hazel recognized her from the old photograph.

"Hailey," she greeted, extending her gloved hand. "Welcome home."

Hailey ducked her chin, fingers twisting in her scarf. "Feels strange hearing that. I wasn't sure I'd ever make it back."

"David's getting you checked into the inn," Hazel said gently. "But first—there's someone who's waited thirty years to see you."

Hailey's breath caught.

"He's at the lake. We thought you might like... some privacy."

The lanterns flickered gold along the narrow trail, guiding Hailey onward. She clutched her coat tighter, heart hammering. Beneath her scarf, the ruby necklace lay snug against her skin, a reminder of the promise they'd made in another lifetime.

At the clearing's edge, a man stood by the frozen lake, a solitary figure framed by the lights. The years had etched themselves into his face, but the moment he turned and saw her, time folded in on itself.

He stopped short. "Gwendolyn?"

She swallowed twice before she could speak. "Hello, Jeremiah."

For a long heartbeat, the only sound was the faint crackle of ice on the lake.

"It's really Archie."

She untied her scarf. "I'm Hailey."

His attention fell to the glint of red at her throat.

"You kept it." His emotion rough. "After everything…"

She reached up, fingertips brushing the gem. "I wanted to return it. That night, after you gave it to me, I went back to the inn to pack. I thought I'd meet you at the cemetery before midnight, like we planned." Her breath misted in the air, trembling. "But the marshal was waiting when I returned. He said we had to go. No warning, no goodbyes. My family was already packed. We were in witness protection. I wasn't supposed to tell anyone."

Archie took a step closer, emotion tightening his features. "You disappeared. The blizzard hit, the roads closed… everyone said your family stole the necklace and ran."

Tears gathered, bright along her lashes. "I never meant to leave with it. I asked to go back, but the marshal wouldn't let me leave or even write a note. We were in danger. I thought maybe, one day, I could return it… explain everything."

Archie shoved his hands into his pockets. "I waited at the cemetery all night. By morning, they found me half-frozen. I thought… I thought I'd been a fool."

She stepped closer, her own tears slipping free. "You weren't. You were the one thing that felt real to me back then. I never expected you to wait or to lose so much because of me."

He shook his head, a faint, rueful smile breaking through the ache. "Christmas was ruined forever. I stopped celebrating after that night. Couldn't stand the songs, the lights, the cheer. All I saw was the snow and the empty road."

Hailey reached out, her fingers brushing his sleeve. "Then maybe it's time to get it back."

She unclasped the necklace and held it out to him, the ruby catching the lantern light in a burst of crimson fire. "It was never mine. It was a promise. I kept it safe because I couldn't bear for something so full of love to be lost."

Archie's hand closed gently over hers. "You did more than keep it safe."

CHAPTER 34

By nightfall, the whole town had gathered in Willowcroft Square. Gentle flurries glowed under the streetlamps. Strings of lights crisscrossed the rooftops, and the scent of spiced cider and roasted pecans drifted from the vendor stalls.

Tammy and the team found a spot near the front as Wally balanced a tray of steaming paper cups. Sugary steam wafted through the air, mingling with the aroma of pine from the state park.

"Hot chocolate for the victorious sleuths!" he announced, distributing the drinks. "Extra marshmallows for Xander, as requested."

Xander snatched his cup. "You're the best, Wally!"

As they sipped, the carolers began *Rockin' Around the Christmas Tree*, their harmonies adding to the festive atmosphere. Tammy savored the drink's heat and the companionship around her.

"I haven't had this much fun in years." Mrs. T's whole face crinkled with laughter. "Who knew reuniting young lovers could be so invigorating?"

"Exhausting more like it," said Olivia. "But... in a good way."

"I'm not happy we skirted the law, even if it was for a good cause," said Wally. "We're not doing that again."

A sudden lump formed in Tammy's throat. "I never thought... When I came to Willowcroft, I was so lost. So alone."

The others quieted. She rarely opened up.

She continued, her words soft but steady. "My mother always said I'd never have real friends, that no one would ever truly care about me. But you all…" Tammy looked around at each of them, her eyes bright with unshed tears. "You've shown me what family really means."

Mrs. T clasped Tammy's hand between both of hers. "Oh, my dear. You've given us just as much as we've given you."

Wally's shoulders squared. "More, I'd say. You brought us all together. Don't forget that."

The carolers slowed into *Silent Night*, and a quiet glow spread through her chest. For the first time in years, perhaps for the first time ever, she was home.

Before they could say more, a familiar voice piped up behind them. "Oh, goodness gracious. I'm so glad I've run into you all tonight."

They turned to see Margaret Taylor white-knuckling her handbag, a fine sheen of perspiration visible on her upper lip despite the winter chill.

"Margaret," Mrs. T said. "Lovely to see you."

Mrs. Taylor's breath came in short, visible puffs. Her eyes darted toward the post office across the square, then back to their faces, then to the ground. "I… I suppose there's no easy way to say this. I owe you all an apology. I was the one who made that threatening phone call."

"We thought as much," Tammy said.

The corner of Margaret's mouth twitched. Her fingers twisted the handle of her handbag. "I didn't mean to frighten anyone. I just…" She swallowed audibly. "I didn't want my husband to get in trouble for keeping the letters, or both of us, given that I read them all, every single one. I was terrified of what might happen, but at the same time, they became like a yearly Christmas present, better than any romance novel I could have bought. I couldn't stop."

"And I couldn't either." Mr. Taylor stepped forward.

He'd been close enough to hear.

"Truth is, I knew someone had been in the post office with the sill wiped clean and the kettle turned the wrong way. I nearly called the sheriff, but nothing was missing. I assumed it was all of you," he looked around at the team, "but those letters were still right there in the bottom drawer. I couldn't point them out, as I'd have to explain why I'd kept them all these years."

His cap dipped lower. "Technically, I was supposed to forward them to the Mail Recovery Center in Grand Rapids, but no one ever audited us out here, and I never had the heart. They were part of Willowcroft's story by then. Seemed cruel, somehow. When I realized Margaret had been reading them years ago, I figured we'd both already broken the rules. It didn't make sense dragging anyone else into it."

Margaret's eyes filled. "Oh, darling, you knew?"

Before he could reply, a cheer erupted from the crowd, drawing every gaze toward the stage.

There, beneath the towering Christmas tree, stood Archie Beaumont beside his mother, Marion. The stage lights glimmered off the ruby that gleamed proudly at Marion's throat.

A hush fell over the square, followed by murmurs of recognition.

"The Beaumont ruby!" someone exclaimed. "It's been found!"

Marion smiled, her frail hands steady as she touched the gem. "It's home again," she said softly into the microphone, and the crowd broke into applause.

Mr. Taylor stared, astonished. "Well, I'll be... I hadn't heard."

Mrs. T clasped her hands together. "Mr. Taylor, meet Jeremiah."

He blinked. "Pardon?"

Wally rocked back on his heels. "Jeremiah was a code name for Archie. And the woman beside him? That's Gwendolyn."

"You can deliver those letters now," Olivia added. "No auditor will ever know."

Mr. Taylor stood there, his mouth opening and closing like a man trying to catch up with a story thirty years too late. A long exhale misted in the cold.

"I'll deliver them first thing in the morning," he said. "And then I can close the Dead Letter Office for good. I'd say that's a record—thirty years of mail delivered in one day."

"And just in time for Christmas," said Mrs. T.

Mayor Marzolon stepped up to the podium, his red coat a bright splash against the snowy backdrop.

"I missed my cue," said Wally. "Gotta go." He hightailed it to the bell ringer's stand.

The mayor tapped the microphone, and the speakers crackled to life. "All right, Willowcroft! Who's ready to light this tree?"

The crowd erupted in cheers. The excitement swept Tammy along. She glanced at Olivia. "I've never seen so many people this worked up over a tree before."

Olivia giggled, her breath visible in the frosty air. "Just wait. It gets better."

"Let's count it down together!" Mayor Marzolon called out, raising his arms. "Ten!"

The townspeople joined in, their shout rising in unison. "Nine! Eight! Seven!"

Tammy shouted along, her eyes fixed on the massive spruce.

"Six! Five! Four!"

The square plunged into darkness.

Lockie pawed at her coat, and Tammy picked him up so he could see.

"Three! Two! One... Light it up!"

The spruce exploded into life, thousands of lights igniting in a dazzling array of colors. Reds, blues, greens, and golds twinkled against the night sky, reflecting off the market stalls and creating a magical, shimmering effect.

"Merry Christmas, Willowcroft!"

Marion shone beneath the glowing tree, the ruby necklace blazing, fire captured in glass.

A collective gasp rippled through the crowd, followed by thunderous applause. Tammy stood transfixed, her mouth agape. It was like something out of a movie, but better because it was real.

"Oh, wow." She was unable to tear her gaze away from the spectacle. "It's... it's beautiful."

Lockie meowed in agreement.

Warmth radiated from the people surrounding her. Laughter and excited chatter filled the air, and a surge of contentment washed over her.

She pressed closer to Olivia. This was what Christmas was supposed to feel like. Not the plastic trees and fake snow of LA, but this genuine, shared joy. For the first time in years, she was here. Present. No deadlines, no plot twists, no mother's cutting remarks, no cheating boyfriends, no missing manuscripts, no friends who would betray her.

Olivia's elbow bumped her side. "You okay there? You look a bit misty-eyed."

Tammy blinked. Tears stung her eyes. "Just taking it all in. I think I finally understand why people make such a fuss about white Christmases."

With the spruce glittering behind him, Wally raised an ornate bell and called out, "Time for some good old-fashioned bell ringing. Who's ready to make some noise?"

The townsfolk cheered. Tammy had never participated in anything like this before.

"Here," Olivia said, pressing a small silver bell into her hand. "You'll need this."

As the church choir began to sing *O Christmas Tree*, Wally raised his bell high. "On three, everybody! One... two... three!"

The air erupted with a cacophony of bells, ranging from tiny jingles to deep, sonorous tones. Tammy shook her bell enthusiastically, laughing as Lockie swatted at it.

"This is chaos!" Tammy shouted to Olivia over the din.

"Isn't it great?"

As the song progressed, Tammy found herself singing along.

When the final notes faded, Wally took charge. "Official bell ringers, with me! We've got a trail to light!"

Bell still in hand, he led a small group toward the state park.

Olivia's fingers locked around Tammy's wrist. "Come on!"

A winding trail was lined with unlit lanterns, stretching as far as she could see into the darkness.

Wally and his team spread out. At his signal, they rang their bells in a rhythmic pattern. As if by magic, the lanterns flickered to life, one by one, creating a glowing avenue through the woods.

"It's straight out of a fairy tale," Tammy murmured. The lights appeared in sequence.

"It's my favorite part." Olivia drew closer to the lanterns.

"Let's explore this enchanted forest!"

Tammy linked arms with Olivia as they strolled down the twinkling path. She pulled her scarf tighter, relishing the crisp winter air that nipped at her cheeks.

"This is so different from LA," Tammy mused. "Back there, it was all palm trees with fake snow and sweating Santas."

Olivia giggled. "I can't even imagine. Was it awful?"

"Not awful, just... not this." Tammy gestured around them. "There's something glorious about real snowfall and these lights."

They rounded a bend, and she gasped. A clearing had been transformed into a winter wonderland, with ice sculptures glittering under strategically placed spotlights. Families gathered, pointing and laughing.

"Tammy! Olivia!" Mrs. T waved from near a sculpture of a massive snowflake. "Come see this one. It's exquisite!"

A lump formed in her throat. Flakes melted on her eyelashes. The world steadied. Maybe perfect wasn't a thing you found but a place you arrived at without noticing.

CHAPTER 35

The crowd dispersed as the bell ringers finished their final round through the light trail. The white glittered under the golden shimmer of candlelight and colored bulbs, and happiness rippled through the trees. Tammy and Mrs. T had wandered off toward the cider van with Xander in tow, Lockie trotting between their boots. A furry marshal keeping order.

Olivia paused at the edge of the clearing, savoring the moment: cardamom and honey, roasting chestnuts, and smoke from the bonfire. She nestled deeper into her scarf, her face tingling from the cold.

A familiar voice emerged beside her. "You're not sneaking off without saying hello, are you?"

She pivoted. Her heart fluttered. Mike stood a few feet away, his jacket dusted with white, dimples creasing his wind-chapped cheeks.

"Just admiring the view," she said. "Though I suppose that includes the scenery."

He chuckled. "Careful, Ms. Huddlestone, flattery will get you everywhere."

Olivia arched a brow. "Is that so?"

They strolled along the twinkling path, the town square lights fading behind them.

"You know," Mike said, his eyes crinkling, "I never thought I'd be grateful for broken windows, but here we are."

Heat flooded her face, but she couldn't resist. "Well, I always say the best relationships are built on a strong foundation of shattered glass and police reports."

Mike shook his head. "Your jokes are worse than my medical skills."

"Hey now," Olivia protested, batting at his coat sleeve. "My jokes are a cut above the rest, thank you very much."

He threw his head back, amusement lighting his eyes.

"You know," she tipped her head in exaggerated contemplation, "I think those broken windows were the universe's way of saying our relationship needed some... pane management."

He covered his face with one hand. "That was terrible."

"Terrible?" Olivia feigned offense. "That pun was positively scrumptious. A real zinger, if I do say so myself."

As they walked along the trail, the teasing dissolved into a comfortable silence. Their boots crunched over the snow, and the twinkle of fairy lights shimmered against the frozen branches. Conversation came easily. No careful, polished phrasing from Manhattan soirées. Just ease and understanding.

"You've gone quiet," Mike said, his elbow grazing hers. "Cooking up more window-related puns?"

Olivia grinned. "Oh, I'm letting those ideas marinate. You never know when inspiration will strike, same as a well-aimed snowball."

Before he could react, she scooped up a handful of snow and tossed it at his shoulder.

Mike sputtered, grinning, as he patted the powder from his coat. "Oh, it's war now, is it?"

"Depends who wins," she teased.

Their eyes held. His arm brushed hers, a whisper of contact tingling her nerves. His breath hitched. *Had he felt it too?*

"So," Mike said, gravity entering his tone, "I hear you're heading to New York soon. Need any help packing?"

Anticipation prickled along her spine. Was he asking to see her again? "That's sweet of you to offer," she said lightly. "But I think I can manage. I wouldn't want to subject you to my chaotic process. It's not for the faint of heart."

He laughed, the sound deep and genuine. "I'm tougher than I look." He flexed his arm in mock bravado. "I can handle a few wayward socks."

They reached a mistletoe-adorned archway draped in fairy lights. Olivia glanced up, the air snagged in her throat. Their shimmer reflected in Mike's eyes, turning them into flecks of gold.

"Well," she murmured, "if you're offering…"

His expression turned tender. He moved into her orbit. "Olivia, I'd like to see you again when you get back from New York. If you're interested, that is."

Her heart soared. "I'd love that."

Flurries drifted down, tiny stars catching the lamplight.

The moment crystallized as Mike drew closer, palm cradling the side of her face, his thumb brushing her cheekbone. Her lashes lowered as their mouths met, and the world fell away. His lips were warm despite the cold, tasting faintly of hot chocolate. When they parted, frost crystals clung to his hair, and her fingertips still tingled where they'd gripped his lapel. Best Christmas in Willowcroft? Without question.

Thank you for reading *Bells, Bodies & Blizzards!*

Can't get enough of Willowcroft?
Check out the bonus webpage for this book.

A novella called **Cemetery, Codes & Christmas**
will be available there.
The QR code will take you straight there.

https://franheapwriter.com/bonus-page-bells/

You'll need the password.

It's the tenth word of the tenth chapter.

Hint: It has seven letters.

Loving Willowcroft?

Why don't you write a review to help other readers discover it.

Click on the QR code to be taken to various review options.

Welcome to Willowcroft

A quick refresher for returning sleuths and a handy guide for newcomers.

The Team

Tammy Rumbelow – Thriller/mystery writer turned cozy mystery writer. New to Willowcroft from Los Angeles since the summer. Lives in the little blue cottage just outside of town. Her last thriller review stated: "She's not just over 40, she's over, full stop."

Olivia Huddlestone – Owner of Bookworm Haven bookstore with a genealogy side gig. Moved from Manhattan 15 years ago after turning twenty-one. Curious to a fault and loves food but can't cook. Lives above her store.

Mrs. Hazel Temperance (Mrs. T) – Retired history teacher, knitting circle matriarch, and widow of the town's late doctor, Harold. Daughter of a British WW2 war bride, Elsie. Born in Willowcroft. Known for her colorful shawls and occasional Britishisms. Lives in the northwest corner of the square in the old doctor's surgery and residence.

Wally – Retired town sheriff with a Boston Homicide background. Divorced with children and grandchildren all living in Boston. Lives three doors down from the north-east corner of the square and the Sheriff's Department.

Xander Simmons – Tech-savvy teen who'd rather code than socialize. Won a teenage comedy night competition at the local radio station. His dad is Park Ranger Dan, who oversees the state park bordering town.

Lockie (Pawlock Holmes) – Tammy's adopted stray cat. An integral member of the team who sniffs out clues that humans miss. A town celebrity after helping apprehend the instigator in the Willowcroft Great Bear Caper.

The Willow-Crafters (Knitting Circle & *Knotty but Nice* group text)

Betty – Romance obsessed. Hazel's best friend since childhood.

Marjorie Hubbard – Stern, prim, and proper. Keeper of the grapevine, though she'd never admit it. Married to Gerald.

Della Mae Beasley – Bit of a hoarder. Married to Roger.

Beatrice Smith – Can't do a slip stitch to save herself.

Other Townsfolk

Nick Bradley – Classmate of Xander's doing Community Service for his summer pranks.

Maxine – Town librarian.

Bev – Administrator for the Sheriff's Department and keeper of the department's archives key. Promised Wally he could access the archives whenever he needed after he solved a cold case that brought closure to a former resident's murder.

Eleanor Bennett (formerly Cross) – Lives in Serenity Gardens care facility, friends with Hazel and Marjorie.

Max Cross – Eleanor's older brother. In a state of advanced dementia prior to his death last summer at Serenity Gardens.

Nathan Cross – Max's grandson, currently residing in a forensic psychiatric hospital.

Mrs. Robinson – Sister-in-law to a skeleton, Cathy, found in the tunnels.

Willowcroft's Town Square Businesses

Bookworm Haven – Olivia's cozy bookstore. Headquarters for sleuthing, featuring a hidden bookcase door and a murder board. Olivia lives in the apartment above. (Nestled between the bakery and diner.)

Sweet Crumbs – The town bakery owned by Mr. and Mrs. Applewood. She is the town hugger and famous for her apple pie, which no one else in town sells.

The Swinging Spoon – A classic diner owned by Peggy Hughes, known for its pancakes and cherry pie.

Mrs. Hubbard's Cupboard – Local grocery store run by the current Mrs. Hubbard, Katie. It was previously run by Marjorie Hubbard, Katie's mother-in-law, and by Marjorie's mother-in-law before that. It's known for providing the best and most up-to-date gossip in town.

Waves of Willowcroft (WoW) – Local radio station. Held a teen comedy competition in the summer, which Xander won. Housed in the basement that once formed part of the Willowcroft Bank.

Willowcroft Bank – Scene of a 1954 bank heist, which has only recently been solved and the money recovered. The building has been subdivided over the years.

The Retro Reel – Willowcroft's old-school movie theater.

Pizza Pasta Pallooza – Local pizza delivery service offering other meals as well.

Vintage Vault – Antique store owned by Mr. Bonavy.

Polished and Teased – Local hair and nail salon run by Vanessa and Bree.

Pippa's Pop Ins – Short-term rental for businesses.

Handy Hammer – Hardware Store.

Off the Town Square

Serenity Gardens – Nursing home/care facility overlooking Parkland Orchards. Nurse Emma is a regular staff member known for her wacky medical scrub designs.

Willowcroft Inn – Only inn in town, run by George and Georgina Gregson.

Willowcroft State Park Campground – Located on the east side of the park, known for its bear sightings. It has a bear cam app.

The Blarney Tap – An Irish pub.

Parkland Orchards – An apple farm where Mrs. Applewood (formerly Parkland) grew up.

Bradley Berry Farm – Known for its blueberries and blueberry honey.

Drive-In – Opened in 1954, located on the road out of town toward the highway and Stonefield.

Towns of Greater Willowcroft

Stonefield – Shopping Plaza, Hospital, Library (its own)

Oaktown – Cozy Corner Cafe

Lakeview – Mrs. Bennett's home from when she married until entering Serenity Gardens.

Pinebrush

Willowcroft Series

www.ingramcontent.com/pod-product-compliance
Lightning Source LLC
Chambersburg PA
CBHW060551190726
48283CB00003B/968